Becky Williams went missing on November 24th, 1971, the exact same day D.B. Cooper vanished up in Oregon and Washington.

But even though that was before Pickett's time on the force, everyone knew this case by heart. Becky Williams had been a twenty-one-year-old college kid, liked by everyone, working in a local restaurant while going to school.

Rich parents, a lot of friends, no reason at all to vanish.

She had lived in the Independence Apartments on the East end of Fremont Street. They were high-end apartments, recently remodeled at the time. Her parents paid for the place and she even had a car.

The Independence itself was a historical building in Las Vegas, built back in the middle Prohibition days when Vegas was starting to boom thanks to the construction of the Hoover Dam. The hotel was said to have had a speakeasy in its basement at one point.

When Becky lived there it had been completely remodeled, keepings its old art deco look while making the apartments modern for 1971, and the basement where the speakeasy was rumored to be was a laundry room for the tenants.

Becky had gone into the building, into her apartment on the second floor, and completely vanished. The building had security, a doorman, and cameras and there was no evidence at all she ever left the building. At least not by normal means.

But no crime scene was ever found and every inch of the building was searched. She or her body never turned up anywhere.

The D.B. Cooper of Las Vegas.

ALSO BY DEAN WESLEY SMITH

COLD POKER GANG

Kill Game

Cold Call

Calling Dead

Bad Beat

Dead Hand

Freezeout

Ace High

Burn Card

Heads Up

Ring Game

Bottom Pair

Case Card

THE POKER BOY UNIVERSE

Poker Boy

The Slots of Saturn: A Poker Boy Novel

They're Back: A Poker Boy Short Novel

Luck Be Ladies: A Poker Boy Collection

Playing a Hunch: A Poker Boy Collection

A Poker Boy Christmas: A Poker Boy Collection

GHOST OF A CHANCE

The Poker Chip: A Ghost of a Chance Novel

The Christmas Gift: A Ghost of a Chance Novel

The Free Meal: A Ghost of a Chance Novel

The Cop Car: A Ghost of a Chance Novella

The Deep Sunset: A Ghost of a Chance Novel

MARBLE GRANT

The First Year: A Marble Grant Novel

Time for Cool Madness: Six Crazy Marble Grant Stories

PAKHET JONES

The Big Tom: A Packet Jones Short Novel

Big Eyes: A Packet Jones Short Novel

THUNDER MOUNTAIN

Thunder Mountain

Monumental Summit

Avalanche Creek

The Edwards Mansion

Lake Roosevelt

Warm Springs

Melody Ridge

Grapevine Springs

The Idanha Hotel

The Taft Ranch

Tombstone Canyon

Dry Creek Crossing

Hot Springs Meadow

Green Valley

SEEDERS UNIVERSE

CASE CARD

A Cold Poker Gang Mystery

DEAN WESLEY SMITH

WMG
PUBLISHING

CASE CARD

Case Card:

The very last possible card in the deck needed to make a hand.

Always for Kris!
Thanks for putting up with my eye issues...

Part One

WE'RE BACK!

CHAPTER ONE

November 24th, 2022
Las Vegas, NV

It was D. B. Cooper Day. November 24th. Retired detective Debra Pickett found that almost funny, in an ironic sort of way.

In front of her, on the white marble kitchen counter, two gold detective badges glowed, looking very out of place. For the past two years and seven months, the badges had been on a shelf near the kitchen along with some mystery novels and a few goofy awards she and Sarge had gotten when still on the force. Those badges had rested there, out of the way, out of sight, and seldom talked about.

Now, of all days, on D.B. Cooper Day, she had brought the badges off the shelf, cleaned them, and put them where Sarge would see them when he came down for his morning coffee.

When she and detective Ben "Sarge" Carson had retired from the force, they had both joined the Cold Poker Gang Task Force, solving cold cases. That was when they had met and fallen in love, which neither of them had ever expected to do again in their lives.

The Cold Poker Gang Task Force met once a week at one of the detective's homes to play poker and talk about cases, but the task force had shut down in March of 2020 in the pandemic and now it was late November of 2022. Wow, that was a long time.

She and Sarge had spent the time together, staying safe, waiting for their vaccinations to finally come around. And even exercising more than they had before the shut-down. One of the fun things they had gotten into over the last two years was celebrating strange holidays.

It seemed that just about every day was a holiday of something or another, and it had become not only a habit, but a lot of fun to try to figure out how to celebrate each holiday.

Now, the day the Cold Poker Gang Task Force comes back into active duty is the day to celebrate the most famous of all cold cases. Maybe Andor, the retired detective who ran the task force, had planned it that way. She doubted it. Just not his style.

She picked up her gold badge and held it, feeling the once-familiar weight in her hand as she shifted it from hand to hand, then put it back on the wide stone counter of the kitchen. She had honestly doubted those badges would ever be moved again except to dust the shelf.

For so many decades that detective's badge had been her main focus in life, and for a couple years after she retired, the badge had been a symbol of her value with the Cold Poker Gang Task Force.

That badge and the Cold Poker Gang Task Force had introduced her to Sarge, the man she could not imagine living without.

Pickett was now sixty-seven and her new husband, Sarge was sixty-eight But both of them were still in top shape and had managed to stay that way, even through the entire pandemic. They had actually gotten married this last summer, even though both of them had originally sworn to never do that again after their first marriages.

While Sarge was still sleeping, Pickett had gotten a call from her old partner while on active duty, Robin Sprague, who had told her the Cold Poker Gang Task Force was firing back up and she had a new case for the three of them from Andor, the retired detective who was its connection to headquarters.

"Same rules and restrictions?" Pickett had asked.

"Nothing changed," Robin said.

"Except the entire world," Pickett said.

Robin made no comment to that.

Pickett pulled up a bar stool and sat staring at the badges for a moment, sipping on her coffee.

Around her, the morning Las Vegas sun filled their massive dual penthouse condo in the Ogden with bright morning light through the two-story floor-to-ceiling windows. At the moment, their three cats were nowhere to be seen. Pickett knew they were in the other half, spread out in the sun over two couches and an ottoman.

For the last two-plus years, she and Sarge had lived very comfortably here, first off ordering in all their food and supplies, then after they both had their first two shots, heading back out to restaurants that were open and struggling, not only to get out, but to try to help the struggling businesses.

And every day they played with whatever holiday it was that day, sometimes learning more about the holiday, sometimes just toasting to it in the evening.

But the daily holiday had become an important ritual over the last few years. And they both thought it weird and funny.

But it was also fun.

And through the pandemic they had needed some fun, and something to focus on even a little.

Now, below the massive windows, the city seemed to be back and growing. Las Vegas had life again and she and Sarge had spent a lot of time seeing shows and finding new restaurants and just enjoying living.

Not once in all that time had they talked about the task force coming back. She kind of assumed it would not.

And to be honest, part of Pickett didn't want to put that badge back on. But part of her did. She wanted to wait and see what Sarge thought before she decided, before she let Robin send her the new case. She didn't want to be tempted by a cold case that was interesting. They had all been interesting over the years in one way or another.

She just sat at the counter, thinking and staring out over the beautiful city and the Strip beyond. Finally, at his normal time, Sarge came down the stairs. His full head of white hair almost glowed from the shower. He was, far and away, the most handsome man she had ever known, and what he saw in her, she'd never know.

She was just glad he saw something.

CHAPTER TWO

November 24th, 2022
Las Vegas, NV

Damn, Pickett looked beautiful sitting at the kitchen counter, smiling up at him. In all his imagination, Sarge would have never dreamed of finding another person this late in his life to love. And he couldn't fathom how he would have gotten through the last two years without her.

This morning he had on his normal jeans, running shoes, and dress shirt tucked in, moving easily, not at all like many his age. He felt in shape, felt loose and almost better than he had felt back in his forties when he had allowed himself to add about thirty pounds.

It was thanks to Pickett that he kept in shape and exercised. He needed to keep up with her.

Their two badges were on the counter for the first time since 2020. He used to live for that badge and loved solving cold cases with the task force. More than likely Pickett was waiting for what he would think about the task force coming back.

He actually felt excited about it, but didn't let himself show it.

He got a mug from the cabinet as he did every morning, poured himself a cup of coffee, then picked up his badge and put it on his belt where he had always worn it before, and then sat down and smiled at her.

She just smiled back at him, shaking her head.

"We're back, I'm guessing."

She just laughed. She should have known there would be no doubt with him. He was like her. She had lived for that badge and what it meant for decades. If he could put it back on, she would. And he had no doubt she would as well.

She reached over and took her badge and hooked it to her belt where she had normally carried it.

"Feels great, doesn't it?" he asked.

"Beyond great," she said. "Not even sure why I had even hesitated."

"We're back," he said, smiling as they toasted with their coffee mugs.

"We're back," she said, leaning over and kissing him after the toast.

"What's the case?" he asked, sitting back and sipping his coffee.

"Damned if I know," Pickett said. "How about we meet Robin for breakfast like we used to do and have her bring the file?"

He and Robin and Pickett had formed a great three-person team on the task force. He and Pickett did all the legwork and interviews, Robin did all the computer work.

"Golden Nugget buffet never reopened," Pickett said.

Sarge nodded. That had been their meeting place for their first three years with the task force. He kind of missed it.

"Main Street Station buffet is open for breakfast," she said. "Not as cheap as it used to be and food is bland, but at least it is back open."

"Perfect," he said, taking a long sip of his coffee and then placing the mug in the sink. "We can walk to it like we used to do to the Nugget. You call Robin, I'll get our guns out of the safe."

"Are we really sure we want to do this again?" Pickett asked.

"I can't imagine not doing it until they shut us down again," he said. "And besides, it's D.B. Cooper Day. What better day to solve a cold case."

Pickett smiled.

Sarge could feel the excitement flow through him for the first time in two long pandemic years.

"I can't imagine anything else either," Pickett said.

And he couldn't. They had made it through the years of pandemic, now it was time to go back to work. After all, that was what they had done for decades.

CHAPTER THREE

November 24th, 2022
Las Vegas, NV

The Main Street Station Casino was located near where the old Las Vegas train station used to be, and was decorated like a 1900s ornate train station, with towering, polished wood columns and massive beams thirty feet overhead. The front desk area even had polished wooden train benches and the front desk itself looked more like a front hotel desk from 1910 than anything modern.

The casino had an old-time feel to it overall, and someone had even scattered old and sometimes expensive antique furniture around. Massive plants dangled from the ceiling and the wooden beams. This was the only major casino in Vegas that actually had windows all around. Most of them were stained glass, but they were windows letting natural light flood over the slot machines.

Pickett always felt comfortable in the place and this morning was no different. The walk was exactly five blocks and the morning wasn't cool enough yet to require more than light jackets to cover their guns. Perfect Vegas fall weather.

Robin sat at a back wooden table under one of the massive windows when they got there, already eating. She looked almost identical to when she and Pickett had been partners. While Pickett kept herself thin and looking like a runner, Robin was always square-shaped and kept her brown hair short.

Robin and her husband ran one of the top security companies in the city, protecting everyone from politicians to major celebs.

Robin waved at them as they paid and then filled their plates before heading to the table to join her. Pickett got her normal eggs and bacon and oatmeal while Sarge did what he always did in a buffet and filled his plate with a half-dozen different forms of meat. Even for breakfast.

"Happy D.B. Cooper Day," Sarge said to Robin as he sat down across from her.

"Happy day to you as well," Robin said, smiling. "And Andor is really playing with us."

Pickett looked at her old partner. She knew that grin on Robin's face. It meant this case had something really strange about it.

"How is that?" Pickett asked as she sat down next to Sarge.

Pickett slid a brown file toward her across the table that had stamped on it, *Copy*.

Pickett glanced at the name on the file.

Becky Williams.

"No chance!" Pickett said.

Sarge glanced up from his plate and Pickett turned the folder so he could see the name on it.

Sarge just shook his head. "Andor is in a mood to restart us, I see."

Pickett just nodded and started into her eggs.

Becky Williams went missing on November 24th, 1971, the exact same day D.B. Cooper vanished up in Oregon and Washington.

But even though that was before Pickett's time on the force, everyone knew this case by heart. Becky Williams had been a twenty-one-year-old college kid, liked by everyone, working in a local restaurant while going to school.

Rich parents, a lot of friends, no reason at all to vanish.

She had lived in the Independence Apartments on the East end of Fremont Street. They were high-end apartments, recently remodeled at the time. Her parents paid for the place and she even had a car.

The Independence itself was a historical building in Las Vegas, built back in the middle Prohibition days when Vegas was starting to boom thanks to the construction of the Hoover Dam. The hotel was said to have had a speakeasy in its basement at one point.

When Becky lived there it had been completely remodeled, keepings its old art deco look while making the apartments modern for 1971, and the basement where the speakeasy was rumored to be was a laundry room for the tenants.

Becky had gone into the building, into her apartment on the second floor, and completely vanished. The building had security, a doorman, and cameras and there was no evidence at all she ever left the building. At least not by normal means.

But no crime scene was ever found and every inch of the building was searched. She or her body never turned up anywhere.

The D.B. Cooper of Las Vegas.

The belief was that somehow she never left the building and now haunts it.

Andor had given them Las Vegas's most famous cold case to bring them back after two years. Pickett had no idea why, other than he somehow knew they were going to celebrate D.B. Cooper Day today.

What the hell, maybe they could solve them both at the same time.

CHAPTER FOUR

November 24th, 2022
Las Vegas, NV

Sarge really loved the feel of the Main Street Station, the stained-glass windows, the huge old beams. The buffet dining room was divided into five large areas surrounding the massive, curved line of food. There had to be a hundred people in the massive place, but the sound was low enough that he and Pickett and Robin could talk easily.

Turned out that after they finished eating and started talking about the case, a reason for Andor's madness came clear.

And why he had wanted them on it today.

It seems the Independence was being remodeled once again into high-end condos this time. It had sat empty and boarded up for almost a decade, but the historical designation for the building hadn't let anyone tear it down.

So now, spending more millions than it would have cost to build it new, they were going to remodel. And today they were tearing out the interior, including Becky's old apartment. So Andor wanted them to be there, see if Becky's body turned up somehow.

To Sarge that made a lot of sense, so after finishing eating, he and

Pickett walked home, put on old tennis shoes, older clothes that wouldn't matter if they got ruined or dirty, and then walked the four blocks to the Independence.

It was surrounded by a high construction fence and had a bunch of equipment hauling out debris from the inside through what used to have been a massive front door.

Robin was just parking down the street and the foreman handed all three of them helmets and then pointed to a guy who clearly didn't look like a construction worker.

"Architect," the foreman said. "He'll show you around."

They introduced themselves to Baker Dunn, who seemed instantly passionate about this ancient old building.

Baker was a young architect as far as Pickett could tell, with slightly longer brown hair and clear skin that made him look younger than she guessed he was.

He had green eyes and they just lit up with the passion of the project in front of him.

"You're going to have to be careful, Detectives," he said. "Some of the old walls and flooring have deteriorated pretty badly. We're tearing it all out as fast as we can, saving what we can."

Pickett admired Baker's passion and his ability to see what was possible from a mold-smelling pile of wood as far as she was concerned. She liked that most buildings in Vegas, when they reached the last of their useful life, were just torn down. Kept the city fresh and modern-looking.

"Are you familiar with the Becky Williams missing person case?" Robin asked Baker.

He laughed. "Anyone around this building for any amount of time knows every detail."

"So can you show us what's left of Becky Williams's old apartment?" Sarge asked.

"I can," Baker said, nodding. "But we got most of the wallboard off and the floors torn up in there. Just no place for a body to have stayed hidden since 1971."

With that he turned and led them through the big archway, around a pile of mold-smelling pieces of wood and flooring, and up a staircase to the right. To Sarge the staircase had almost an old Southern mansion feel to it, sweeping up and curving to the left over the large main foyer. Beautiful, yet at the same time creepy in its ruined state of peeling paint, remnants of carpet, and broken railings.

The hallway on the second floor was lit by a few construction lamps and it led to the left. It was narrow like hallways of the time and Baker led them single file to the second door on the right.

"Stay on the plywood covering the joists," he said as he stepped aside and let them into the apartment.

As Baker had told them, most of the walls were gone, leaving only old studs that they could see through into the apartments on either side.

It didn't take long to see that there was nothing to hide a body. Even the ceiling above was gone, showing the temporary plywood on the floor of the apartment above.

Where a kitchen and bathroom had been only capped off pipes remained.

Sarge nodded, then turned to Baker who was standing in the door. "Can you show us where the old speakeasy was rumored to have been?"

"Sure," he said and started back toward the stairs, leaving them to follow.

The best guess over the last fifty-one years was that somehow she had found her way into the walled off speakeasy and then gotten trapped and died. But in all the years, no one had found where that speakeasy might have been. All the space for it was supposedly used by a furnace room and the laundry room when it was remodeled before Becky moved in.

But with no evidence at all that Becky left the building on the day she disappeared, and her apartment and every apartment being completely searched more than once, only the old speakeasy was left to answer this mystery.

Sarge didn't give it much hope. He actually believed it had never existed.

CHAPTER FIVE

November 24th, 2022
Las Vegas, NV

Baker led them back down the grand staircase, then around and down another regular flight of stairs under the larger staircase. Again, it was lit by construction lamps and the smell of mold and mildew got a lot worse. Pickett had no doubt she would be throwing these clothes away when she got home.

At the bottom was a large room that clearly had been plumbed for washing machines that were long gone. A shelf was built into one wall and was half torn out.

"This was supposedly the main part of the speakeasy," Baker said. Then he moved over to a door and shoved it open, stirring up even more mold and mildew smell if that was possible.

He clicked on a light just inside the door, showing a couple more construction lamps and the remains of a couple large furnaces.

"Here was the back room and supposedly storage for the speakeasy."

Pickett looked around, trying to get herself to imagine this as a hidden speakeasy. The floor was concrete, but the ceiling above was just regular wooden joists.

"Anyone would hear the music from this place through that floor," Pickett said. "It would have never stayed hidden."

She pointed up and Sarge nodded.

So did Robin.

"Speakeasies, at least ones that tried to stay hidden, had to be sound-proof completely," Robin said.

Baker just sort of looked puzzled which gave his young face an inno-cent look.

"My bet is that the speakeasy was below this concrete floor," Sarge said. "But how come no one in fifty years has found a way down into it?"

"Pretty certain there is nothing down there," Baker said.

"Not thinking like a criminal," Pickett said to Baker, smiling.

Sarge laughed. "I knew there was a reason I married you."

"You married me? I remember I married *you*."

"Kids," Robin said, shaking her head. Then she turned to Baker. "You run ground-penetrating radar on this floor?"

He shook his head. "Saw no reason to."

"So," Sarge said to Baker. "Could you get some of your crew down here to pull down some walls and see if we can find a staircase down."

He nodded and headed back up the stairs while the three of them slowly explored, looking for something that residents of this building and detectives had missed for fifty years.

Yeah, fat chance of that.

Baker brought the three of them face coverings, commercial grade for the dust that was about to be stirred up.

Then two of his men set up three heavy-duty fans to blow as much of the dust that was going to be generated back up the stairs.

And two other men brought down a large flexible pipe, large enough for a person to crawl through and sat that up pumping in fresh air. When everything was started it felt like a windy day in the basement.

Pickett thought that very strange, but was very glad they did it.

"Any idea where you would like to start, detectives?" Baker asked once everything and everyone was ready to go.

Sarge pointed to the built-in shelf and stepped back with Pickett and Robin to the other side of the room.

The crew made quick work of the shelf, kicking up as little dust as possible as two other workmen carried the wood up the stairs and out. Pickett stood beside Sarge and Robin and just watched. She had a feeling about this. Not a good feeling.

Behind the shelf was a wall that looked original to the building and Baker indicated that his men should tear it out as well.

Once the dust cleared enough to see what was behind the wall, and in the wall, Pickett knew they were on the right track.

Baker had his men stand back and he moved over and directed his flashlight between the old studs of the wall on what looked to be frayed rope and a giant counterweight sitting on the base of the wall. Pickett guessed that weight weighed as much as she did, if not more.

Pickett looked at it and said, "I think we just figured out what happened to Becky Williams."

Sarge nodded. "The rope broke."

CHAPTER SIX

The rope seemed to vanish over the top of the wall. Sarge knew, just as they all did, that the counterweight had been used to open and close a very heavy door into a soundproof speakeasy below them.

But where was that entrance? And why hadn't anyone seen it in all the searches of this basement?

Baker gave his men a break and the four of them stood staring at the large counterweight in the wall.

Sarge looked over at the open stairs leading upward and then at the ceiling above them. Neither of them would block that much sound.

"So if sound was critical," Pickett said, "the door can't be in this room."

"Is that door original to the building?" Sarge asked Baker, pointing to the door leading into the back storage area.

"It is," Baker said. "The remodeling in the late 1960s didn't move it."

"So with that door closed," Pickett said, "it would offer some sound protection when the door to the speakeasy was opened."

"It would," Baker said and all four of them moved into the next room over.

The floor there was also old concrete and the walls also looked to be concrete. There was a door on the other side of one of the old furnaces.

"That go up a back staircase?" Sarge asked, pointing at the door, and Baker confirmed that it did.

"So either the speakeasy entrance or a service entrance or both," Robin said.

Pickett and Sarge both turned around to face the open door to the old laundry room.

"That rope vanishes up into that area," Sarge said, pointing to an area behind the open door.

Pickett moved over and closed the heavy door with a thud. It clearly had not been closed in decades and she had to really push it over the floor to get it closed.

And the moment she did, that room got even more frightening. Before it just smelled, now it felt dangerous.

"The large counterweight was used to help lift something," Sarge said. "So look for a door near here in the floor."

Sarge was about to give up as all four of them spent the next ten minutes studying everything on that floor until Pickett said, "Here."

She was pointing to an area behind the door they had closed.

It took Sarge a moment to see it, but the door wasn't really a door, it was a half-door in the wall and a half-door in the floor. Kind of like a regular door had been bent in half.

Sarge had no idea how that would work, but once they brushed the dust out of the cracks in the floor and on the wall, it seemed strange enough to be possible.

Baker suddenly got excited. "Only seen pictures of these out of Europe," he said. "The wall portion slides back and up into the wall."

He showed the motion with his hand in the direction it would go up.

"This lower part should slide down and sideways under the floor, revealing a staircase down right here."

He looked around. "There should be a way to move those slabs from this side without destroying them, even without that counterweight that would move that top slab up."

"Imagine a raid on this place," Pickett said. "It couldn't be anything a cop might trigger accidently."

"And it would have to be close and accessible when the door was closed. This would never work with that door open."

Sarge immediately went to the back door trim and carefully ran his fingers along it until he said, "Got it."

He tried to pull what seemed to be a lever down, but couldn't move it.

"Need a small crowbar or hammer and more than likely a few of your men."

Baker nodded, opened the door back up to the staircase and the other room, much to Pickett's relief, and got the tool and three men.

When they were all back inside, he again closed the door and handed Sarge a claw hammer.

Sarge got the hammer behind the metal lever and pulled it down and with a grinding sound the small section of the floor moved aside showing the top of a step down.

A dry rotting smell came up from out of the hole.

"There is another lever here, but going to need two or three of your men lifting on that wall there as I pull it."

Three of the workers lifted as Sarge pulled the lever hidden on the trim behind the door and the piece of wall lifted with a horrid grinding sound and vanished.

"Okay," Sarge said. "Someone put some nails in those levers to hold them in place," pointing to the area behind the door.

One of the workers stepped to do as Sarge asked.

"Can we block up that wall and block the entrance open so it doesn't close up?" Sarge asked. He had no desire to be trapped with whatever was down those stairs.

Baker nodded to another of his guys and pointed to the back door and the guy went out that way.

"And we're going to need full oxygen masks to go down in there," Robin said.

Again, Baker sent a worker to get them.

While they were waiting, standing above the open staircase, Pickett couldn't believe they had found this place. Granted, it was stunningly well hidden, but fifty years of looking and remodeling, someone should have found it.

Baker sort of answered her question for her.

"You know," Baker said, shaking his head. "I would have remodeled this entire building, including this basement and never once known that room was down there. More than likely it is as large as this entire basement."

"Got a hunch," Pickett said, "there is more than a room down there."

CHAPTER SEVEN

The workers got the two slabs blocked open and another fresh-air hose like the one on the staircase pumping fresh air in through the back door while fans blew out the bad air.

"Gloves," Robin said and for the first time in years Pickett put on crime scene gloves.

"We can't touch anything at this point," Sarge said. "If Becky is down there, we're going to need an active detective to come on scene and finish all this."

"You okay with this?" Pickett asked Baker and he nodded. No doubt there wasn't a chance in the world as an architect he was going to miss this, dead body or not, and no matter how pale he looked.

Pickett glanced around to make sure the other three were masked up, then she carefully started down the stairs with her cell-phone flashlight on.

It was clear that this staircase was made for regular customers, more than likely in dress clothes because it widened out almost at once.

And the room beyond was like a picture out of time. A long wooden bar filled the wall to Pickett's right, with a good twenty ornate barstools in front of it and hundreds of bottles on the back bar, all made of identical brown glass. Most still looked full.

A good twenty ornate wooden tables surrounded by cloth chairs filled the center of the room on black and white patterned tile, and on the far wall was a bandstand with instruments still in their stands and an empty wooden dance floor in front of the bandstand.

The walls were covered with drapes and art and posters from the 1930s. Everything was just frozen in time.

Pickett got to the bottom of the staircase and moved to one side to let the others join her. She could hear her own breathing in her ears inside the mask. And she knew almost instantly she was feeling shock.

The shock wasn't from stepping back ninety years in time, but from the scene at one table in front of her, near the bar.

There were five mummified bodies slumped either on the table or on the floor by the table.

All of them had an empty shot glass of whisky in front of them, and there were two of the unlabeled brown bottles from behind the bar on the table.

One of the women was dressed in the clothes Becky Williams had last been seen in. And her hair was the right length and color.

"Looks like Becky Williams was having a party," Sarge said.

"And with tainted forty-year-old moonshine," Robin said. "Clearly that stuff killed them quickly. None of them even made a move for the door."

"I think I'm going to be sick," Baker said.

Sarge turned him and hustled him back up the staircase as fast as they could go.

"I'll call in the active detectives," Sarge said as he left.

Pickett managed to turn away from the death scene. She was very glad she had the mask on. Chances are the room wouldn't smell of death, but of mold and dust and with the bodies that was even worse.

To the right of the end of the bar was a door and Pickett and Robin moved over and opened it.

It was a storage area full of shelves and shelves of booze in the same exact brown bottles. The shelves filled the wall behind the bar and filled the rest of the room like library shelves. A lot of booze and not much else.

"Seems on our first day back not only have we solved Becky Williams's missing person's case," Robin said. "Just as we all thought, she was in the speakeasy. But now we got four others. Just got to figure out who they were."

"Yeah," Pickett said. "Won't that be fun?"

Robin laughed, but Pickett knew that with Robin and her husband's computer skills, she would have the four identified very quickly.

Pickett and Robin went back out into the big room frozen in time in the 1930s and stopped for a moment to take one last look at the room and the bodies slumped around the table. It was just amazing, an image of art almost, a very real representation showing how many deaths Prohibition had caused.

Only these deaths happened 38 years after Prohibition ended.

"Not sure I'm ever going to forget this one," Robin said.

"Yeah," Pickett said. "An amazing first day back."

"Got that right," Robin said.

Then, as they turned for the staircase, Pickett asked, "Do you think there's any chance that one of those guys with Becky might be D.B. Cooper?"

Robin laughed and then said, "After all this, it wouldn't surprise me in the slightest."

Pickett also laughed. "Yeah, I agree there."

Part Two

NEVER EASY!

CHAPTER EIGHT

January 18th, 2023
Las Vegas, NV

"They're turning the Becky Williams case back over to us," Pickett said as she hung up the phone.

Sarge was standing at the kitchen sink sipping on his coffee. He just nodded.

"Going to meet Robin back at the Main Street Station for breakfast to go over the files the detectives put together from the last two months."

Sarge knew that Robin had been in regular contact with Andor and it seemed the dead bodies in the speakeasy had all been identified, and the cause of death was poison on all of them, as suspected. The rub was that the poison had been added to the bottles by someone. It had not been the old booze gone bad that had killed them.

They all had been murdered, including Becky Williams.

And Sarge bet it was by someone who had been drinking with them.

And no one seemed to have a clue who killed them all. Let alone why. So Sarge knew this day would come eventually that they would get the case back as a cold case, and at times over the last couple of months he and Pickett had talked about it.

Solving a fifty-one-year-old multiple murder was not going to be easy, to say the least.

Sarge moved over and sat at their kitchen counter to drink his coffee. Around them the sun filled the massive main room of the condo, making the white counters brighter and the tan furniture almost glow. He loved this place, and especially sharing it with Pickett, who before they had met on the Cold Poker Gang Task Force had been his neighbor. And when they decided to live together, they got permission to punch an archway between the two massive penthouse condos.

So now they had an obscenely large place that gave their three cats lots of room to run, that was for sure. And a lot of space that neither one of them used.

The day outside was a cold winter's day in Las Vegas, which meant the temperature would top out in the 50s. The sky was blue, but the sun had no heat with it, and there was a slight wind. So they both put on what they called their "winter coats" which for back East would be a light spring jacket. Then they headed out for the five-block walk.

Sarge never seemed to mind the cold on his ears and face and hands, while Pickett had on a stocking cap and thick gloves.

Even with the cold, the walk was easy and enjoyable and Sarge loved watching the tourists in their shorts and thin shirts shivering because someone had told them it was always warm in Vegas.

Robin was at what was quickly becoming their table in the back of the Main Street Station buffet. Over the last two months they had met here a dozen times on other cold cases, but this morning, getting this mass murder case back felt different.

Sarge and Pickett paid, filled up their plates and joined Robin.

Without pausing eating, Robin slid the thick folders toward them and Sarge opened the top one which was the main case file as Pickett poured them coffee.

Inside the front cover of the folder was a bright color image of the scene in the hidden speakeasy. And what struck Sarge instantly was the empty chair at the table with the bodies.

The table had six chairs and five bodies.

The detectives had gotten no prints that didn't belong from any of the glasses or bottles and extra DNA had not survived the fifty-one years.

He put the file between them and both he and Pickett slowly worked through the main parts as they ate.

The poison was common, had been common since the 1800s, simple to get in 1971, not so much in 2023. It could be given out in drops, so it would have been easy and quick to poison the two bottles. The poison was fast-acting and from the report the five never really realized what was happening.

If there had been a killer with them for that sixth chair, the killer knew enough to wipe anything touched down.

No wonder the active detectives slid this back to the Cold Poker Gang Task Force in just two months. There was nothing, flat nothing, to go on.

They had solved Becky Williams's missing person case, but Sarge doubted they would be able to solve her murder.

CHAPTER NINE

January 18th, 2023
Las Vegas, NV

Pickett just shook her head as she finished scanning through the main file. Fifty-one years was a very long time.

"How come no one put these five missing people together before now?" Sarge asked, indicating the five files on the table, all with a different person's name on them, including Becky Williams. "Didn't see that in the summary file."

"No reason to," Robin said as she finished the last bite on her plate and pulled two very thin files from the pile. "Kevin Donnally and Katie Stevens, both nineteen, newly married, sophomores at Boise State College. They were on their honeymoon, stopped in Vegas to see friends at the college here, and were only reported missing two weeks later when they didn't return home to Boise as planned. But no one knew where to start looking for them."

"Was Becky one of their friends they were stopping to see?" Sarge asked.

"No connection the detectives could find," Robin said.

Pickett glanced at the high-school graduation pictures in the files of two fresh-faced young kids. They should have had the last fifty-one years of life, kids, and grandkids.

She closed the files and moved them aside. She had a hunch she would have nightmares about those faces.

Robin moved another file forward. "Rusty Buhl, twenty-two, assistant golf professional for a few weeks at the Dunes Country Club. Actually his job was fetching carts for the members and he was known to be upset with the job, so no one at the club reported him missing when he didn't show up for work."

"Family?" Pickett asked.

"Two half-sisters up in Montana, both still alive, both always wondered what had happened to him, but no one was close to him that the detectives could find."

The picture in the file was of a sun-tanned young man with short blond hair and a large grin, taken with a golf course behind him.

"The last victim at the table besides Becky was Connie Carlson," Robin said, sliding the very thin folder across the table to Pickett. "A couple years older than Becky at twenty-three and clearly the same social level with money."

"Detectives could find no connection I assume," Sarge said.

"None," Robin said. "Connie, as far as anyone reported, was last seen in San Diego five days before the murders happened. Parents dead. She had a brother in Chicago she called every week or so to check in and he sent her money from the trust fund for them when she needed it."

"Reported missing?" Pickett asked as she stared at the picture of the young woman smiling in a glam shot of some sort or another.

"Brother reported her missing in Chicago and then five years later had her declared dead and got her share of the trust."

Both Sarge and Pickett looked up at Robin, who shook her head. "Detectives followed that one. Brother put his sister's share of the trust into another trust in case she showed up and all the money is still there, actually considerably larger than when he started the second trust."

"Nothing is going to be easy about this, is it?" Sarge asked.

"Nothing," Robin said.

Pickett could only stare at the folders and shake her head. She was sixteen when this happened. Just the age of this crime seemed impossible to climb over.

That and any lack of clues.

CHAPTER TEN

January 18ᵗʰ, 2023
Las Vegas, NV

The sounds of the Main Street Station buffet washed over the three of them as they sat silently, just staring at the brown folders on the table. Sarge could not remember another case since they had started with the task force that had so few clues.

And none they had dealt with was this old.

Finally, he just decided to follow what the active detectives had done in the last two months and see what came up.

"So the actives on this one tried to figure out that sixth chair and if a person was in it. Am I right?"

"They did," Robin said, nodding and tapping the big main file. "They chased a bunch of leads and got nowhere."

"Considering the intense focus on the Becky Williams case," Pickett said, "it's amazing none of these five were recorded going into the Independence. At the time that place had great security."

Sarge suddenly felt a spark of excitement. Just a spark, but it was enough. "So how did they get in?"

Robin shrugged. "Back basement door."

Pickett set up straight, smiling. "That door was bolted from the inside and locked and according to Becky Williams files, it had not been tampered with."

"And the building had a doorman stationed just inside the front door," Sarge said, "and would have seen all these people going down the main staircase. Becky might have slipped past him without being noticed, but not five other people."

"The speakeasy had another entrance," Robin said softly.

"More than likely a tunnel so that when the building entrance and back door was being watched by the Feds, customers of the time could come and go."

"Have I said how much I hate tunnels," Pickett said.

Sarge just laughed. After some of their cases over the first three years with the task force, he wasn't fond of them either."

"I'll call the architect, Baker, and tell him we are on the way," Robin said.

"Give me thirty minutes for dessert and another cup of coffee," Sarge said, standing.

"A man after my own heart," Pickett said, smiling and standing with him.

"I'll tell him an hour," Robin said as the two of them walked off toward the desserts arm-in-arm like two teenagers.

CHAPTER ELEVEN

January 18th, 2023
Las Vegas, NV

Pickett and Sarge went back to their condo in the Ogden and got gloves, warm hats, and flashlights, then Sarge drove his Cadillac SUV to the site of the construction on the old Independence historical building. On a warm day, they would have still walked, but with what they were looking for, no telling what they might need.

Robin was already there and was standing waiting with Baker Dunn. For over a month before the holiday his work had been shut down due to finding the bodies, and he had given the entire crew the holidays off, so they had only been back at work for just over two weeks. So actually, to Pickett, it didn't look like much had gotten done.

And she knew that he had standing orders by not only the police, but the state historical society to not touch anything in the speakeasy. In fact, the cement slab doors had been closed after the bodies were removed and twenty-four-hour guards put on the place.

"You tell him what we are looking for?" Sarge asked Robin as they approached.

"Now what?" Baker asked, a slight panicked look on his young face.

"A tunnel into the speakeasy," Robin said. "By any chance do you have a map of this neighborhood when the Independence was originally built?"

"I do," Baker said. "Including pictures of her in the beginning. The owners and I are trying to take her back to that old art deco look as much as we can."

He led them to a small travel trailer parked to one side and climbed inside. He quickly found the pictures and a map and spread them out on a fold-down table.

The trailer was tight with all four of them in there, and it was warm. Not stifling as Pickett might have guessed, but comfortably warm. It looked like a typical construction trailer with mud smearing the floors and everything labeled, but it smelled wonderfully of coffee with a slight hint of hot chocolate in the background.

Baker first showed them pictures of the original Independence. It really was a stunning building, built in 1925 far enough away from the old Fremont Street and train station to be fashionable. It was just off to the side of Fremont Street where that street basically became the Boulder Highway leading out to the construction of the Hoover Dam.

The original Independence had a beautiful lawn and hedges around it, and it even had a pool, unusual for the time. There were only a few homes that they could see in the picture around it. Mostly just empty desert outside the lush green grounds and East Fremont Street a block over.

Pickett just shook her head. "This is far too much in the open to have a speakeasy in it. Too easy to watch those coming and going and raid the place."

"Agreed," Sarge said, and Robin nodded.

"What's the closest hotel?" Sarge asked.

"In nineteen-twenty-five when the Independence was built," Baker said, "the closest buildings besides a few ranch homes were eight blocks to the west up Fremont Street with the original hotels and such there in those original downtown blocks. The train station was a long ten to twelve blocks. Guests would be driven from the train station to the hotel."

Pickett looked up at Sarge beside her. He clearly was considering the same thing that she was. Somewhere down there was a ten-block or longer tunnel.

So after looking at a few more maps and pictures, Baker gave them helmets and led them back into the construction. He had two of his men follow them downstairs into the concrete basement and to where the levers were to open the concrete doors to the speakeasy.

"I was told to expect you," the guard in the basement said, nodding as Sarge flashed his badge. He was fairly young and way overweight. But he looked like he cared about his job.

"No problems?" Pickett asked him.

The guard just shook his head. "As it should be."

Baker had two of the men open the cement slabs and then nail the levers open.

"Air is all cleared out down there," Baker said. "And been tested, so no need for masks. But we are not allowed to touch anything."

Pickett nodded along with Sarge and Robin, and with their phones on flashlight, they headed down.

Baker led the way and at the bottom he moved to a switch and got the place lit up with construction lamps he had strung along the ceiling.

For the first time, Pickett noticed how high the ceiling was, and the two huge crystal chandeliers that filled the center of the room. With modern lighting, the place just looked old and dusty, more like a picture of a ruin from the past.

And now the dust smell covered everything.

The poison bottles and glasses had been removed from the death table and the chairs arranged like the other dozen or more tables in the room. All the tables had six chairs around them.

The wall of brown bottles on the shelves behind the bar had two empty spots where the poisoned bottles had been taken.

The bar was wood, very wide, with mirrors behind shelves on the back-bar area and the identical brown bottles filling those shelves. The mirror on that wall and on the wall around the grand staircase made the room feel even larger than it was.

Pickett didn't feel much about the room this time. It was a historical snapshot of a period long gone, and at the same time a crime scene from yet another time period.

"This place is just amazing," Baker said, his voice hushed. "There has been no other speakeasy this well preserved ever found."

"I wonder what caused the sudden shutdown?" Robin asked. "As if the employees one night cleaned up, expecting to come back, and then just never did."

"Even to get their instruments," Sarge said, indicating a trumpet on a stand, a small set of drums, an alto sax on another stand and an upright piano that looked like it was made of cherry wood.

"This place must have really rocked," Baker said, clearly lost in his own images and knowledge like a kid in total awe.

Pickett could feel under the murder scene the same awe. The cloth wall-hangings were of scenes from ancient Greek or Roman times and must have had bright colors in their time. They were now faded and a few looked like they were about to come down to expose the cinderblock wall behind them.

Those hangings would have muffled the sound a lot.

"So how would people come into here for a night's party?" Sarge asked. "We know they could not have come down those stairs, or very few of them because of the location of this building in the desert."

Pickett agreed. "Those stairs were clearly for guests of the hotel. Everyone else had to come in a different way."

Sarge and Pickett both moved past the bandstand into an alcove between it and the bar. The lights that Baker had set up didn't reach the alcove that well, so they both pulled out their cell phones and clicked on the flashlights.

Just more cloth-covered walls. The cloth looked rotted and covered in dust. Pickett was afraid of even touching it.

There was a small two-chair table against the back wall, but as Pickett knelt down to look under the table, she realized that both the chairs and the table were floating above the floor, attached to the wall.

"This wall moves," Pickett said.

Behind her she heard Baker say, "What?"

"In or out?" Robin asked.

Sarge pointed the powerful flashlight from his phone at the ground.

"No scratch marks, so it would go out."

With that he carefully put his hand near the edge of one of the hanging cloth wall decorations and pushed.

And frighteningly, without a sound even after all the years, the wall and table and two chairs just swung outward.

CHAPTER TWELVE

January 18th, 2023
Las Vegas, NV

Sarge and Pickett each grabbed a chair from in front of the bandstand and braced open the wall so it would not close again on its own. Then Sarge stepped through into a room that also had high ceilings with chandeliers, cloth tapestries on the walls just as the speakeasy, and a dozen more tables and chairs of the same kind as in front of the bar. The floor was a decorative white and black tile that just felt it was from the 1930s.

Clearly, on a busy night, Sarge had no doubt that the wall could be braced open and this would be an overflow room.

"Wow," Pickett said, right behind him, shining her light around as well. "This place was huge."

Sarge nodded. The two rooms together made this speakeasy the size of a large ballroom. This might be the biggest speakeasy on record. Typical Las Vegas to never do anything small.

He waked through the tables and chairs to a wide tile staircase leading downward. From the beam of his light, he could see that almost two flights of white tile stairs down became a wide wooden tunnel going straight ahead that looked a lot like a mineshaft, but very, very wide and what looked like poured concrete for a floor.

Pickett and Robin came up beside him and added their flashlight beams down the stairs.

"With the band playing and that wall open," Pickett said, "you would be able to hear the music a long ways in that tunnel."

"And this second hidden room," Robin said, "could be used to hide in case the place was raided from the hotel side. Really smart."

The entire room smelled stale and Sarge bet the air was stale and not at all healthy.

"We need supplies and help before we go any farther," Sarge said.

"No argument there," Pickett said. "I'm betting we also need masks."

Together, they turned and Sarge took the stunned architect by the elbow and led him back through the speakeasy, past the death table, and back up the stairs.

Outside, out of the way of the construction, in the cold Vegas winter air, they all stopped. Sarge was glad to take a few deep breaths. That air in that room had been stale since at least 1971, when the murderer more than likely went out that way.

"In relation to the building," Robin asked the clearly shocked Baker, "where is that second room?"

Baker pointed straight down. "A good twenty-five feet under us right here."

"So still on the property?" Pickett asked.

Baker nodded.

Sarge turned and pointed back up Fremont Street. "Tunnel heads in the direction we suspected it would. West, right into the center of town"

"Amazing," Robin said, shaking her head.

Sarge turned back to Baker. "We need oxygen masks again."

He nodded.

"And does your surveyor use GPS?"

Baker nodded. "All modern surveyors do for various things."

"Think he would be up for exploring a tunnel in about thirty minutes? Tell him we think it goes under Fremont Street all the way to the old hotel district."

"I will call him and ask," Baker said, pulling out his phone and stepping away from the three of them.

"We also need The Cowboy," Pickett said. "I'll call him and see how long he will take to get down here."

She pulled out her phone and stepped away in the opposite direction from Baker.

Both Robin and Sarge nodded, standing there taking in the cold, fresh air.

The Cowboy, as everyone called him, was Kip Cantrell, one of the world's leading experts on mine shafts, their construction, and their safety. Nevada had thousands and thousands of miles of mostly old mine shafts. Everyone called him The Cowboy because he saved and raised wild horses on his massive ranch to the north of the city.

Pickett clicked off her phone and stepped back to Sarge and Robin. "He's actually in town just finishing an early lunch and will be here with equipment in fifteen minutes. He sounds excited."

Sarge nodded, then glanced at Baker as he finished his phone call.

"Fifteen minutes," Baker said. "I'll get the oxygen masks."

"Four of them," Sarge said. "Robin, we need you and Baker on the surface because if we actually can get through this tunnel, no telling the problems we will find on the other side in a basement area of one of the old hotels."

Baker looked relieved and turned to go get the masks.

Robin nodded. "Good plan. I'll get all my team on the ready and doing research on the time period and the hotels working at that time, including a couple lawyers on speed dial. We'll dig up as much as we can about the old hotels along Fremont from 1925 to when Prohibition ended."

"Add in 1971," Sarge said, "since I'm betting our victims and killer came in that way from a hotel then."

"Well, this will be an adventure," Pickett said.

Sarge just smiled at the woman he loved. He didn't say that they would have to live through it all for it to be an adventure. But he had no doubt that Pickett was thinking just that.

CHAPTER THIRTEEN

January 18ᵗʰ, 2023
Las Vegas, NV

Pickett smiled as The Cowboy strode toward them from his panel van. He had four hardhat helmets with lights on them under one arm, two coils of rope over his shoulder, and a pack full of who knows what slung over his other shoulder.

He gave Pickett a full bear-hug without dropping anything, then smiled at Sarge and shook his hand. The Cowboy was as tall as Sarge at just over six foot, but had huge shoulders and arms and almost looked square. His face was ragged from too much weather and sun and he looked older than both Sarge and Pickett, even though Pickett knew he was barely over fifty.

The Cowboy had this personality that everyone loved and he had done more to save Nevada's herds of wild horses than anyone. To Pickett, The Cowboy just seemed larger than life.

The Cowboy nodded approval to the oxygen masks and then handed each of them a helmet and put another one on. "I'll get my own oxygen from my van. This tunnel that long and deep?"

"More than you can imagine," Pickett said, "and not opened since 1951 and the 1930s before that. Built in 1925 for a speakeasy."

"Oh, shit," he said. "When I heard you two had gotten hitched, I expected the world to explode. So this is what I get in exchange."

He shook his head and turned for the van.

Both Pickett and Sarge laughed. They both, while active-duty detectives, had worked with The Cowboy a number of times. And they both liked him. A month after their wedding, they called him and took him out for a fun dinner and drinking. He drank how he lived life: Hard, fast, and with relish of every drop.

Ten minutes later The Cowboy was back, when a thin guy carrying a stick with an instrument on the end of it joined them.

Baker introduced him as Bill Stickler, the surveyor on the Independence remodeling project.

"Call me Stick," the young man said as he shook everyone's hands.

Pickett just smiled at that. Sometimes nicknames just fit and this one really fit the thin kid with jeans, running shoes, and a dress shirt with the sleeves rolled up. Even though the rest of them wore coats and Pickett could see her breath in the cold air, Stick didn't seem to mind or even notice the cold at all.

"I hear we might be headed for the downtown area underground," Stick said, "so I loaded in the maps and underground maps of the area into this as well as all the elevation above sea level. The GPS should give us an approximate depth under the surface as we move along. We need more data, I got it in my phone."

Pickett was impressed and The Cowboy said, "Fantastic!"

"How deep will this work?" Sarge asked.

"Says over a hundred feet of rock," Stick said, shrugging. "Never tested it."

"So get an elevation of this point right here?" Sarge asked. "We'll use it as a base point."

Stick put the point of the rod holding the computer-like instrument in the ground and looked at the screen on the device at the top and nodded, pressing a button on it. "Locked in. It will also show us our path and I can print it all out when we get finished back at my office."

"This will keep us in touch in case the phones don't work." The Cowboy handed Robin what looked like a walkie-talkie of some sort.

Robin nodded and Pickett felt relieved. Now they could get fast help if they needed it. She very much doubted their phones were going to continue to work.

Five minutes later, Baker and Robin had escorted them down through the construction to the basement and then down the stairs and into the speakeasy.

All Stick and The Cowboy could say was "Wow!" And at almost exactly the same moment with each new thing they saw.

Pickett understood what they were feeling completely.

CHAPTER FOURTEEN

January 18th, 2023
Las Vegas, NV

Sarge glanced at his watch. It felt late, but actually was just after eleven in the morning. Amazing they had gotten this far this fast today.

"Stick," Baker said, getting to a spot in the second room. "We are almost directly under the spot above. Any idea how deep we are?"

Stick set the rod firmly on the tile floor and then studied the instrument on top of it.

"Without using more precise ways of measuring," Stick said, "I would say right at 25 feet under where we started."

Baker nodded. "About what I thought."

Sarge also nodded and headed for the top of the stairs leading from the second room down into the tunnel.

The other five joined him.

"We'll report in every five minutes once we start into the tunnel," Pickett said to Robin.

"Watch yourselves," Robin said.

The Cowboy laughed. "Nothing's going to happen while I am in charge."

With that he started down the stairs, right down the middle.

Stick followed him.

Sarge and Pickett went to the right side of the white tile stairs where a handrail had been attached to the wall and followed them down. Sarge might be in good shape for his age, but a tumble on uneven and old stairs could spell the end of that. No point in taking stupid chances. They were doing enough of that by thinking of going into a ninety-year-old tunnel.

It was lighter than Sarge expected at the bottom, and he glanced back up at the figures of Robin and Baker above, watching. They looked like they were a long ways above them.

The Cowboy was doing an intense study of the large wooden beams inside the tunnel, mostly just shaking his head as he moved.

"We are almost fifty feet under the point above," Stick said.

"If we head toward the downtown area are we going to run into anything this deep?" Sarge asked.

"Really doubtful," Stick said. "I show nothing under thirty feet on the maps, so it would have to be something built before the maps I have, and they go back to the 1950s."

"Something like this tunnel?" Pickett asked.

Stick just nodded.

"How is our air quality?" Sarge asked.

Cowboy stopped and pulled out some sort of phone-like instrument from his pocket and slowly turned around.

"Fine at this point," he said. "Stale but nothing harmful. I'll keep it on and it will sound an alarm if things start to turn."

"Want me to carry that and monitor it?" Pickett asked.

The Cowboy nodded and handed her the device, showed her how to change the screens to monitor the CO_2 levels and oxygen content and any other toxins that might be in the air.

"So is this place safe structurally?" Sarge asked.

"Safer than most New York subway tunnels," The Cowboy said. "Let me show you."

Pickett waved at Robin as the four of them stepped inside the dark tunnel and all of them turned on their helmet lights, giving them a surprising amount of clear light.

"The wood posts and beams were meant to make this look like an old mine. And the wood siding from the beams down to the floor was put in to give this a hallway feel."

Sarge looked at everything and into the distance this wide tunnel did look like a hallway of sorts.

"But behind all this wood is a concrete tunnel," The Cowboy said. "And only being ninety-plus years old and in this dry climate, this would pass a modern inspection for safety if they rewired all the lighting."

The Cowboy pointed to lights set on the top of every beam that would have lit up the entire tunnel in indirect lighting.

"This would have been an easy walk all times of the year from downtown to the speakeasy," Pickett said, her voice hushed.

Sarge completely agreed. This entire massive speakeasy and this tunnel were really amazing. He would have thought that after an entire life living in Vegas, nothing about this town could surprise him.

Yet this did.

CHAPTER FIFTEEN

January 18th, 2023
Las Vegas, NV

Pickett checked the air conditions of the tunnel just about every ten steps like she was waiting for an important call. They stayed stable.

After about two hundred steps the tunnel turned slightly to the left and The Cowboy stopped them.

"Air conditions?" he asked.

"Stable," Pickett said, checking the device one more time.

"Makes sense," The Cowboy said. "Feel the slight breeze?"

The three of them shook their heads. Pickett didn't feel any breeze at all.

The Cowboy stepped back behind them, reached up and brushed some of the thick dust off the beam.

They all four watched as the dust fell to the ground slowly, but clearly toward where they had come in.

"It would make sense this would be ventilated," The Cowboy said. "Clearly most of the ventilation shafts have been covered, but not all of them."

"We are holding at fifty feet underground," Stick said, "and now are headed west right up the middle of Fremont Street with this slight turn."

"Where under Fremont Street?" Sarge asked.

"Maryland Parkway that crosses East Fremont is about a half block in front of us."

"So off we go," The Cowboy said. "Pick up your feet to keep from stirring up too much of this dust. Cleaning lady won't be in for some time."

Suddenly Pickett realized what The Cowboy said.

"Hang on," Pickett said, and everyone stopped.

She glanced at Sarge and then said, "Footprints."

She moved quickly past The Cowboy and shined her helmet light directly on the undisturbed ground in front of her.

Sarge joined her after a moment and then The Cowboy added his light from a very low angle to show ridges and bumps in the dust with shadows.

"Five sets of prints going toward the Independence," Sarge said. "I can't believe we didn't see them before now. And it would make sense if Becky Williams joined the group from the hotel side."

Pickett was trying to ignore the prints headed away from the city. What she wanted was that one set going back.

And after a moment she spotted it. A woman's shoe print, clearly in heals, headed toward the downtown.

She had been one of the five in the initial bunch, but she clearly went back alone.

Must have been a hell of a walk after just killing five people.

"A woman," Sarge said, shaking his head.

"Let's get a lot of pictures of these on all our phones," Pickett said. "And at different places up ahead. And at some point we are going to need to try to carefully go past on one side to preserve original prints in an area."

Pickett reported in to Robin and told her what they had found and that their killer was a woman. Then they spent the next five minutes taking hundreds of photos from all angles, including numbers showing the woman heading back toward the casinos with the other prints, including hers, heading toward the speakeasy.

Pickett wasn't sure what she was the most shocked about, a woman in heels killing five people in 1971, or that they had found this kind of clue in a tunnel under Fremont Street.

Stick recorded exact location of where they had taken the photos and then with another check of the air quality, The Cowboy led the way toward downtown Las Vegas. They all stayed to one side of the tunnel to preserve as many of the footprints as they could.

After a bit Pickett stopped looking at the prints in the dust. They just felt too much like ghost prints.

And except for one, they were.

CHAPTER SIXTEEN

January 18th, 2023
Las Vegas, NV

Sarge had walked the distance of Fremont Street hundreds of times, but never in a tunnel fifty feet under the street. It just seemed so much longer, and they could only see so far ahead of them with their lights on their helmets.

The faint footprints in the dust from 1971 remained most of the way and Sarge felt like he was destroying crime scene evidence with every step, even though they had everything well documented and were staying single file on the left side of the tunnel to preserve what they could.

Finally, The Cowboy called a halt and pointed at a wooden door in the left side of the tunnel wood paneling as they faced the downtown area. There were no footprints in the dust around it and the door was small enough that Sarge might have walked right past it without even noticing.

"Where are we?" Pickett asked Stick a moment before Sarge could.

After a moment Stick said, "On the West side of the Las Vegas Boulevard intersection with Fremont Street."

Pickett contacted Robin. "There is a door, not used, off the south side of the tunnel on the west side of Las Vegas Boulevard. Going to need to see what was near there when the Independence was built."

"Got it," Robin said, her voice loud in the tunnel.

"Got that marked on the record?" The Cowboy asked Stick.

"Got it as good as the GPS ever does."

The Cowboy nodded and turned toward the Fremont Street Experience fifty feet over their heads. Sarge had a hunch they were going the entire distance under all the tourists.

The Cowboy spotted two more doors in the next two blocks, also unused by the victims and killer from fifty-one years ago. At each door they contacted Robin and Stick gave her an approximate location.

Finally, the tunnel came to an end in a wide area.

"We are right in front of what is now called the Golden Gate Casino and Motel," Stick said. "Still a consistent fifty feet under the surface."

The footprints of the five headed for the Independence and the woman's prints headed away turned to the left and went down a narrower brick-walled tunnel.

Pickett called Robin. "We are in front of the Golden Gate and the only way out seems to head in under the hotel."

"We are ahead of you," Robin said. "Already heading into the basement. We got a search warrant, but the manager of the hotel and casino is working with us willingly and shocked that something like this could connect to his place."

The Cowboy nodded and moved into the brick tunnel, carefully inspecting it. Sarge was glad to stay out into the relatively safer feeling large tunnel while he worked.

After a long minute, the Cowboy nodded. "It's solid."

"So now where do we go?" Pickett asked.

"Real good question," Sarge said.

CHAPTER SEVENTEEN

January 18th, 2023
Las Vegas, NV

Pickett stayed a good five paces behind The Cowboy as he eased forward, checking all the walls and ceiling with each step. Clearly something about the brick he didn't like, but wasn't saying.

She kept checking the air quality. In the smaller tunnel she could feel the slight breeze from in front of them which seemed to hold the air quality in the narrow tunnel in safe ranges.

After about fifty paces, the tunnel ended in a wooden door. They had not climbed at all, so having this wooden door fifty feet underground just felt creepy, as if enough of this wasn't creepy already.

There was a square barn-like handle on the door that was clearly meant to be pulled. And the original black color had been worn from wear. Pickett had no idea how many thousands and thousands had used this tunnel over the years to get to that speakeasy.

"Fingerprints on the handle," Sarge said.

The Cowboy nodded and studied the door and the frame for a moment, then just reached out and with the tail of his shirt, pulled the door toward him slowly from the top edge, trying not to stir up too much dust.

The door seemed to open fairly easily and his light through the door showed a tiled staircase in a large square room.

They all stepped inside and stared upward. The staircase was wide, made of black and white tile like the tile in the speakeasy, and had a landing every ten steps, turning and continuing up for what seemed like a long distance into the dark.

Dark metal railing protected the inside and along each wall was a handrail as well. It looked more like it came out of an old mansion than an underground staircase.

"Robin," Pickett said after she checked the air quality in the staircase room. "We found a large tile staircase heading upward. We are going to need fingerprint techs down here after we get out to dust it all, including the door handle and railings."

"And an elevator," The Cowboy said, pointing to a wide nook in the side of the staircase room opposite. On the rusted old metal Pickett could see the word "Otis."

"That has to be the first elevator in Las Vegas," Sarge said, moving over to get a closer look with The Cowboy.

"And an elevator," Pickett said to Robin.

"An elevator?" Robin asked, sounding as shocked as Pickett was feeling.

Pickett glanced around. Stick was taking measurements and looking at his GPS device and shaking his head.

Finally he turned to Pickett. "Tell them that by my rough calculations, we are fifty feet inside the main casino door to Fremont and fifty feet under that point."

Pickett repeated that information and Robin said after a moment, "We are moving toward that location. The manager has two hotel maintenance workers with us in case we have to tear into something, and Baker is here as well to watch for safety issues."

"Headed up," Pickett said.

She glanced around at Sarge and The Cowboy and Stick.

"Got your climbing shoes on?" she asked. "Don't touch the railings."

And then she stepped aside to let The Cowboy lead and inspect the stairs and walls as he went.

CHAPTER EIGHTEEN

January 18th, 2023
Las Vegas, NV

Sarge was winded slightly by the time they reached the top of the three flights of stairs that had nine landings. He knew Pickett had checked the air conditions with each flight and they didn't seem to vary. But clearly the air was a little thinner than he was used to. Either that or he had a lot of dust in his lungs from that tunnel. He would bet it was a combination of both.

The top of the stairs was more like a wide landing with a wide door painted white and gold and the top of the elevator shaft to one side of the landing with a metal grate across it.

The Cowboy again inspected the door, then being cautious to not hurt any fingerprints, just pulled it open.

On the other side was the back of a stud wall and a small wooden door.

If Sarge had to guess, that wall was built right about when Prohibition ended and the speakeasy was shut down. More than likely their killer had found that small wooden door from the other side and unlocked it.

The Cowboy tried the door, but it was solidly locked.

He then knocked on the wall beside the door.

"We can hear you knocking," Robin's voice came loud and clear through the radio. "Keep knocking and we'll get to your location."

The Cowboy kept up a study pace of two knocks, then a count of five, then two more.

"What do you see on your side?" Pickett asked.

"Nothing but a cinderblock wall the entire length of this side of the basement storage area."

Sarge could hear Robin's voice not only through the radio, but on the other side of the wall in front of The Cowboy.

"You found us," Pickett said. "We are directly in front of you on the other side of that wall."

Through the wall Sarge could hear someone order that part of that wall be torn out. And he could hear Baker telling them how to do it safely.

For the next five minutes the top of the old staircase was filled with the sound of hammering until finally he heard someone say, "There is a wall and a door back here."

Then more hammering until finally on the other side, "Can you open the door?"

"Locked," Pickett said loudly. "But save the handle and lock because it will have our killers prints on it."

"Understood," Robin said clearly from the other side of the door.

In a few moments a power saw cut around where the lock in the door was and it was carefully removed into the other side.

And then Robin pulled open the door, smiling.

Sarge could feel himself smiling as well as they all stepped into the clearly thicker air of the casino basement.

Strangest hour-long walk Sarge had ever taken.

Part Three

DEAD ENDS

CHAPTER NINETEEN

Four days after their hike under downtown Las Vegas, a lot of things had happened, but they had still made no progress on the case and that frustrated Pickett more than she wanted to say.

The State of Nevada and the Historical Society for the State had swooped in and put up protections on everything that had to do with the speakeasy, including the tunnel and the area in the basement of the Golden Gate Casino. And it seemed they had changed the state history with the discovery of that old elevator.

Researchers had discovered that the speakeasy was simply called Independence, the name of the high-class hotel it sat under. And with researchers from the state and historical society and even the Mob Museum scouring the records, no one had come up with the builders of the tunnel.

It seemed, by anyone's best guess, that the wealthy owners of the Independence Hotel had struck a deal with the owners of the Nevada Hotel (that became the Golden Gate Hotel many owners later) and that was that.

When the four of them had gotten out of the tunnel, Sarge had first called Andor and told him what had happened and within thirty minutes two active detectives were on scene with the top forensic unit in the city.

No fingerprints at all on the door or anywhere along the tunnel. All wiped down where anything could have been touched by the woman that they were assuming had killed everyone.

And they knew the woman's shoe was a size six, but no make on the high heel at all.

And worse yet, Robin and her team had scoured the records of the old hotel and no woman besides cleaning staff worked there at all in 1971. None. No dealers, no management, no woman on the corporation board or offices that owned the hotel.

None.

Clearly no woman with easy access to that basement in 1971.

And either by coincidence or purposeful, that cinder-block wall over the old wall had been built that same year, shutting off anyone else using that tunnel and finding the bodies.

So after three days, the active detectives were done, the forensic unit was done, and the case was once again given back to them, just as cold as when they got it the first time.

Sure, they had found Becky Williams. And solved four other missing person's cases. And found a gold mine for the historical society of Las Vegas to exploit.

But nothing else.

From what it looked like, some woman in 1971 had killed five people and then vanished, leaving only her shoe prints in the dust.

So for breakfast, Pickett and Sarge walked down to the Main Street Station buffet to meet Robin and go over where they stood on the case. Pickett knew the answer to that.

Nowhere.

The January day was overcast, unusual for Las Vegas, even in the winter. There was a slight wind from the north and even though the temperatures were in the low 50s, both she and Sarge had on heavy coats and she had on a stocking cap and gloves.

They pretty much made the five-block walk along Ogden Street to the buffet in silence.

As usual, Robin had beaten them and was already eating. They paid, dropped their coats off at the table and this morning not only did Pickett grab her normal eggs and bacon, but added some French toast to the plate covered in syrup and grabbed a dish of bread pudding from the dessert counter on the way back.

Since the buffet had huge stained-glass windows, the dull overcast sky outside seemed to wash the entire restaurant in gray, and the sound of the big dining area sounded muted, even though there was the normal hundred or more people spread out over the massive space among all the plants and soaring beams.

Of course, Pickett's mood about the case didn't help either.

Robin glanced at Pickett's bread pudding and smiled, indicating the slice of key lime pie beside her mostly finished plate of eggs and hash browns. No wonder they had worked so well for so many years as partners.

"Okay," Sarge said as he slid his plate of meat onto the table and sat down. "I got an idea on how we focus on this going forward."

Pickett and Robin both looked up at him.

"Oh, please," Robin said.

"We can't assume the woman killed them all," Sarge said. "There may have been yet another person there, or someone who joined from the apartments above after she left."

Pickett just shook her head and dug into the eggs. It was bad enough when they actually had a suspect. Now Sarge was suggesting that they didn't really. And he was right.

"So instead of making this worse," Robin said, "what do we focus on?"

"The why," Sarge said. "I want to know why those people got together in the first place in that hidden speakeasy in 1971. What connected them all?"

Pickett nodded and kept eating. She had wondered that same thing the first time she saw the bodies, but then with finding the extra room and staircase, that had not come back into focus for her. Clearly it had for Sarge.

"And what I really want to know is how, and more importantly why, Becky Williams ended up with them," Sarge said.

Robin was nodding.

Pickett was nodding as well.

At least they had something they could do and they already had a vast amount of information on Becky Williams to start their search. Suddenly the grayness covering the room seemed to push back just a little. But she was still planning on eating the bread pudding.

And maybe a piece of pie as well.

CHAPTER TWENTY

January 24th, 2023
Las Vegas, NV

Sarge was glad that Robin and Pickett had liked how he wanted to change the focus to why the victims were there. But he was convinced they were not going to like his next idea.

The glass behind the bar in the speakeasy had bothered him, as well as the glass to one side of the staircase. More than likely it was nothing more than design features, but in the last few days he had done a lot of reading about different kinds of speakeasy bars around the country built during Prohibition and more often than not, they all had hidden rooms.

He and Pickett and Robin needed to find that hidden room. It might have more answers, or more than likely more problems.

Or maybe it didn't exist. They had to find out.

"We have to go back down into the speakeasy," Sarge said.

Pickett had a forkful of eggs halfway to her mouth and she stopped and just stared at him.

"Why?" Robin asked, her question not at all friendly.

Sarge did not blame her at all. Last thing he wanted to do was go back down there as well. But they didn't really have a choice at this point.

"Been reading about the designs of speakeasy bars around the country," Sarge said. "Most have hidden rooms."

Pickett dropped her fork on her plate. "The damn mirrors. Stupid things bothered me the first time I saw them."

Sarge nodded. "If there is another room down there, it might hold the clues we need as to a motive."

"Or nothing," Robin said.

"Worse," Pickett said. "More bodies."

"Or nothing," Sarge said, going with Robin. "That is more than likely."

"I'll call Baker," Pickett said, taking her phone out of her jacket pocket. "Tell him we're coming back and need to go down into the speakeasy again."

Robin just shook her head. "He's going to love that. Make it an hour. I got desserts to finish."

Sarge took his phone out of his pocket and called a number he had only put in the phone yesterday.

When a woman answered, he said, "Dr. Heidi Crocket?"

"Yes," she said.

"My name is Sarge and I'm a retired detective working with the Cold Poker Gang Task Force."

The woman's voice perked right up, got brighter and less business-like. "You and your partners are the ones that found the speakeasy and then the tunnel? We will be forever in your debt."

"We are the ones," Sarge said. "But since we are focusing on who killed the people found in the speakeasy, we need your help in about an hour if you are available."

"I am," she said, her voice lower and very serious. "What can I do for you?"

"We need your expertise in speakeasy design in general," Sarge said. "We believe there may be a hidden room down there that has yet to be found."

Silence for a moment on the other end. Then she said, "The glass, of course. Those stupid mirrors. I'll meet you there in one hour."

"Thank you, doctor," Sarge said.

She had hung up so fast, he wasn't sure if she heard that last line.

CHAPTER TWENTY-ONE

January 24th, 2023
Las Vegas, NV

Pickett loved the idea of focusing totally on the victims to figure out, if possible, after all the years, what had brought them all together in that hidden speakeasy. And how they had all gotten in there.

And why someone had wanted them dead.

But she now hated the idea of going back down into that ghost-filled place again. Her gut sense told her that what they were going to find in a hidden room was not going to be something they would like.

Las Vegas has a lot of hidden secrets, especially from the 1950s into the late 1970s when the very last of the mob was finally pushed out. If the existence of that hidden speakeasy was known in that period to certain people, no telling what might be in a hidden room.

And she was even more bothered by how it seemed the place had just been walked away from. Musicians of any time didn't leave their instruments and not come back for them unless something really bad had happened.

And suddenly.

Prohibition ended in December 1933, but everyone knew it was coming. It was not sudden.

She and Sarge talked a little bit about the chance of a hidden room on their walk back to the Ogden where they got in Sarge's Cadillac and headed for the Independence. One-way mirrors had been around since 1900, so by the time the Independence was built, they would have been known and common.

Again it hadn't looked like the construction on the remodeling of the Independence had made much progress and Robin and Baker and a woman dressed in jeans and a heavy parka stood talking as Sarge parked out of the way and she and Sarge joined them.

The day was still just gray, more like Seattle weather than Las Vegas, only so far there was no rain. But for Vegas, it was cold and the slight dry desert wind really cut through Pickett's coat and hands.

The woman introduced herself as Dr. Heidi Crocket from the Mob Museum. Pickett knew she was running point on the entire discovery of the speakeasy for the state and other historical entities who had an interest.

At first glance with the blond hair tied back and almost pure white skin, Pickett thought her young, no more than mid-twenties, but after two or three minutes Pickett kicked that estimation up into her mid-thirties. The woman was sharp and all business.

And she and Baker seemed to be getting along at a level that suggested a little more than a few working visits.

"When I heard we were looking for hidden rooms in the speakeasy," Baker said, "I pulled up the structural footprint of the Independence and then overlaid a floor plan I had done of the main room of the speakeasy, the storage room, and the secondary room out to the tunnel."

He handed each of them a piece of printer paper.

"Faint black lines are the structural foundation plan of the Independence," Baker said.

Pickett could see it clearly.

"The regular lines are the walls of the speakeasy, the staircase from the basement, the doors and the location of the bar and bandstand."

Pickett could see that as well.

"The speakeasy was built to use the foundation walls of the hotel,"

Baker said. "Only the additional second big room and the staircase down to the tunnel is outside those foundation walls."

"So these big empty spaces behind the bar and near the staircase might be rooms?" Robin asked.

Baker only shrugged. "They might be, but they might be nothing but mechanical space or structural columns. Seems we are about to find out."

Pickett just stared at the huge empty space behind the bar that ran the entire length of the bar between it and the storage area. Her stomach was twisting.

"We need to wear crime scene gloves," Pickett said. "And Baker, have one of your men bring some oxygen masks with us."

Everyone just sort of turned and looked at her.

She shrugged. "We already found bodies down there. Just better safe than sorry."

Heidi laughed and nodded. "It is Vegas after all."

"You say that a lot?" Sarge asked.

"More than you can imagine," Heidi said, shaking her head. "More than you can imagine."

CHAPTER TWENTY-TWO

January 24th, 2023
Las Vegas, NV

Sarge led the way down into the old speakeasy under the Independence. He was starting to really hate this dusty old ruin.

In his imagination he could still clearly see the five mummified bodies around the table. They had died in 1971.

Now they were looking for hidden rooms behind one-way mirrors behind the bar and to the left of the stairs. Those rooms had more than likely been closed off since Prohibition ended on December 5, 1933.

His worry was that a lot of people knew about this place from 1933 to 1971, more than likely fewer and fewer as each year passed. But just as with their killer from 1971, some knew how to get down here and maybe into those back rooms. Not only was the speakeasy a perfect place to hide things, but those back rooms, if they existed, would be special.

And that worried Sarge more than he wanted to let on.

As he hit the bottom of the stairs and stepped out of Pickett's way, and the others behind her, he turned on the lights Baker had rigged up.

Pickett looked as worried as he felt. Baker and Heidi both just looked excited. This place was their baby now, and Sarge had zero doubt that the two of them would make sure generations going forward would be in awe of this slice of history.

Sarge just hoped what they might find in the back rooms didn't dampen that excitement.

Pickett and Robin headed into the back storage room, making sure that the door was jammed open behind them.

Sarge, Heidi, and Baker followed them and they all spread out along the wall against the back of the bar, looking for any way in.

One-way glass, or one-way mirrors, worked so that on one side it was bright, while on the other side dark.

So Sarge stepped back into the speakeasy and walked along the bar, looking into the mirror.

The mirror stopped at the far end of the bar and there was a good fifteen feet from the bar to the wall between the main room and the expansion room with the stairs to the tunnel. Fifteen feet with no mirror.

That would be where the entrance was.

He walked back around the bar and into the back room where Baker had set up bright lights and had them turned on the wall behind the bar. The wall was covered in shelves full of mostly unlabeled old brown bottles of booze. He had no idea why every bottle in the place looked pretty much the same, only with a different colored cork. He would ask Heidi later if that was normal for speakeasies.

Sarge motioned for Pickett to follow him and they went to the far end, so deep in the storage room that the light was a lot dimmer.

Sarge got out his phone and turned on the flashlight and Pickett did the same. He studied the floor, looking for any old scratch marks under the thin layer of dust. It didn't take long before he found them.

He pointed them out to Pickett as well and she nodded.

"Found it," she said to everyone. "Gloves on and masks on."

Everyone did and as soon as Sarge had his gloves and oxygen mask on, he turned to the shelf full of bottles and gently pulled.

At first nothing happened, so he pulled a little harder, trying to get the shelf to swing out as the scratches on the floor showed that it did.

Finally the shelf swung open and back against another shelf. It was so smooth that even after all the years, the bottles didn't even hardly move.

Behind the shelf was a black, empty room about eight feet deep and eight feet wide. Sarge had seen bedrooms smaller. Three of the walls were painted black and a black curtain was one wall leading to the area behind the bar.

Sarge clicked on his flashlight again and looked back at everyone. Now they all looked worried behind their masks, just as he felt.

Moving carefully, he stepped inside the square room and then gently eased the curtain back to keep down as much dust as he could and hooked the black curtain on a hook screwed into the wall for that purpose.

Dust was swirling in his flashlight beam, but he still had a pretty good vision of the long, almost hallway-like black room behind the one-way glass behind the bar.

The entire back wall was painted deep black so nothing could be seen through the mirrors from the main room.

The light coming in through the one-way glass colored everything a dark gray.

And thankfully, there were no bodies.

But there were shelves under the glass from the one-way mirror all the way to the floor. Maybe five shelves total and they ran the entire length of the room.

And the shelves were covered in stacks of banded bills.

Completely covered.

Sarge moved down deeper into the long room to give room for everyone behind him.

"Don't touch anything!" Pickett said loudly through her mask.

Near the end of the long room, Sarge leaned down and shined his light on some stacks of bills.

They were all old. From before the end of Prohibition.

So whoever was running this place knew all this money was here, and yet never came back for it. And the musicians never came back for their instruments.

Why had this hidden room with a vast amount of money remained hidden for ninety years?

What the hell had happened on that last day of the Independence speakeasy?

A mystery in 1933 and murders in 1971.

Nothing about this was going to be solved quickly.

If at all.

CHAPTER TWENTY-THREE

January 24th, 2023
Las Vegas, NV

Pickett led the way back out into the main room of the speakeasy at the foot of the stairs and took off her mask.

"There has to be millions back there," Baker said, clearly shocked.

Heidi just nodded and didn't say anything.

Pickett was feeling a little shocked as well, but mostly relieved that there were no new bodies. The money was going to be a problem as to who owned it. Looked to her like the owners who were remodeling the Independence just got a huge boost in their budget. But no telling what would happen when the state and historical societies got involved.

She just wanted to know why all that old money had gone untouched. A number of people must have known about it in 1933. What happened to them?

Sarge had wandered over to the bandstand and, without touching them, was studying the instruments there.

She went over to join him and he pointed to the sax. "This was a well-loved and cared-for instrument. It would not have been left behind without something happening to the owner."

"Agreed," she said. "And that much money would be a great motivator to get rid of people who knew about that room. Including the band that played here every night."

Sarge nodded and turned to look at her.

He was worried, exactly as she was feeling.

"Not liking what we are going to find in that second hidden room by the stairs," he said as they both turned back to the other three.

Pickett could tell that Robin was as worried as she and Sarge felt.

"You two might not like the contents of the second hidden room," Pickett said to Baker and Heidi.

"You thinking more bodies?" Baker asked.

"Musicians and whoever else knew about that back room," Pickett said. "Hope like hell I am wrong."

Both Heidi and Baker nodded.

"Then let's find it and get this all out in the open," Baker said.

They again all headed into the back room and it didn't take long for Baker to spot the marks on the floor where a shelf was pulled open.

Everyone automatically put on their masks and Pickett helped Sarge swing open the shelf.

It latched open and Sarge carefully pulled back the black curtain and hooked it, then stepped inside to get out of the way.

Pickett was shocked. The room was a lot bigger than she had expected, going clear in under the staircase and it only had three chairs in it, each one facing a one-way mirror.

And on the back wall was a rack of guns that could be covered by a black curtain, mostly rifles and shotguns from what Pickett could tell. Shockingly, they were all still there.

One mirror under the stairs looked into the men's bathroom, a second mirror also under the stairs looked into the woman's bathroom, and the third mirror looked into the main bar area.

Chairs were facing each mirror.

"Security room," Baker said through his mask.

"Almost all speakeasies of the time had them," Heidi said, nodding.

Pickett glanced up at Sarge and even with the mask she could see the relief in his eyes.

Same relief she was feeling. No bodies.

Part Four

ANSWERS AND MORE QUESTIONS

CHAPTER TWENTY-FOUR

January 30th, 2023
Las Vegas, NV

Monday morning broke clear and cold, and the sunlight had no real power to it, unlike in the summer where that sun felt like you were getting hit with hot irons.

Sarge had his heavy winter coat on and zipped up under his chin. Beside him Pickett had on her ski parka, gloves, and a stocking cap. For some reason, the cold of the desert never seemed to bother his ears or hands as it did Pickett, although in a cold wind he had been known to wear a hat.

No wind this morning. And the snow on the mountains around the city was spectacular in the sun. So far it had been a good winter for rain and snow for Las Vegas. They needed it.

They were headed to breakfast at the Main Street Station Casino and Hotel buffet, walking along Ogden Street in downtown Las Vegas from their penthouse condo in the Ogden Condominium complex.

Usually this walk was filled with tourists, or locals headed to work in one of the downtown casinos, but this morning he and Pickett basically had the sidewalk to themselves.

Five-block walk at most, but today it seemed longer because of the cold and also the fact that both of them were discouraged at the lack of progress on the Becky Williams murder.

Their kitchen table in their condo had been taken over by papers, files, research printouts, and maybe a hundred yellow sticky notes stuck to things and the table and even one wall near the kitchen counter.

This case was consuming them, more than any other case they had tackled together.

Now they were going to have breakfast with Robin and hope her computer team had had better luck.

But now on a cold case that went back over fifty-two years, there just wasn't much legwork to do, besides what they had already done in finding the speakeasy and the tunnel. And Sarge had no desire to go back into either the speakeasy or that tunnel.

To Sarge, the last days of that speakeasy made no sense at all. The end of Prohibition had put it out of business. But something worse had happened to those who had worked there. But what?

And that was ninety years ago. How did all that money stay hidden and basically forgotten, from the looks of it?

Nothing about any of this made any sense.

As normal, Robin had beaten them to the buffet and already had a plate of food and was at what was quickly becoming their standard table in the back. It kept them away from tourists overhearing their conversations, which was great. Talking about mummified bodies and missing people never did much for normal tourists' appetites.

Because of the huge windows and high ceiling of the buffet, the winter sun made the place feel like they were still outside. Almost cheery, if Sarge had been in a better mood.

They paid, dropped their coats at the table, nodded to Robin, and went and got food. If they continued to not make any progress on this monster case, Sarge decided this might be a two-dessert morning.

After the three of them talked about the weather for a few minutes, finally Pickett said, "No real progress on our side."

"None," Sarge said. "But we did eliminate a dozen ideas on how Becky Williams and the other four that were killed with her ended up down there. Not a connection that we can find with any of them."

Robin nodded. "We have had no luck with that either," Robin said. "But at the moment we are doing some family DNA searching to see if any of them happened to be distant relatives."

Sarge nodded. He gave that no hope, but it made sense to do.

"We dug up Becky William's college classes as well," Robin said, "and worked on cross-checking anyone who took a class with her."

"Bet that took a chunk of time without any leads," Sarge said, digging back into his plate of salty ham, sausage, and a dry slice of prime rib. Someday he might actually walk by the salad part of the buffet, but he doubted it.

"We did have some luck," Robin said, "tracing back the ownership of the Independence."

Robin slid a slim file toward Sarge and he opened it between him and Pickett.

Family that had owned the place were named Sanderson. They had money from the Atlanta area and it was the oldest son, Horace Sanderson, who came west and built the Independence.

He ran it from the time it was built to 1935 when he was killed in a car crash. He had not married and was known as a playboy and gambler with an angry temper when drunk.

His family had the body shipped back to Atlanta and sold the hotel to a group out of LA who ran it into the ground during the years of the Hoover Dam construction. It went through a few other owners until it shut down in the 1960s and then remodeled into apartments right before Becky Williams moved in and then vanished in 1971.

"So his sudden death might explain why the money was forgotten," Pickett said.

Sarge was nodding and thinking the same thing. But that left the question open as to what happened to the band and the rest of the employees of the speakeasy who might have known about the money?

Ninety years was a long time to figure out an answer to that question.

CHAPTER TWENTY-FIVE

January 30th, 2023
Las Vegas, NV

Pickett kept staring at the thin file about Sanderson and his death. A lot of people knew about that speakeasy, how to get into it, and yet that knowledge seemed to have died off or was mostly forgotten by the time Becky Williams went missing in 1971. Sure, the rumor of the old speakeasy remained, but everyone figured the remodeling of the Independence into apartments turned the speakeasy into laundry and a furnace room.

But someone knew enough to get into the tunnel from the Golden Gate basement and Becky knew enough to get in through the basement door. Or someone in the group of five had opened it for her from below. That was more than likely.

So that person was a connection to when the speakeasy shut down in 1933. Almost forty years. The killer might have been a granddaughter of someone who worked at or partied at the speakeasy.

But then that came right back to the question of why kill those five people? And why go to all the trouble to do it so it was unlikely they would ever be found?

Pickett was about to close the file on Sanderson when it dawned on her that if Sanderson wanted to eliminate anyone who knew about the money, she and Sarge were right in thinking he would do it in the speakeasy.

He had not, but that did not mean he didn't do it in the tunnel.

Damn, they were going to have to go back down there again.

Damn, damn, damn. Last thing in the world she wanted to do. But they had to. At least into the tunnel from the hotel side. There were three doors along the tunnel they had seen and gone past. Where did the doors go and what was back there?

Pickett was now betting there were bodies behind one of the doors. At least one.

Pickett looked up at her long-time partner, Robin, and asked, "Do you have what was above those three doors in the tunnel?"

Both Robin and Sarge frowned at her, but then Robin nodded and opened up her laptop.

"First door never had anything above it. Las Vegas Boulevard covers it now," Robin said. "Second door you passed would have gone up under the old Apache Hotel and Casino. Third door under one of the old hotels that used to stand where the Circa now stands."

"You thinking the employees and band might be behind one of them?" Sarge asked.

"I do," Pickett said. "When Sanderson died, all that money was forgotten, that means anyone who knew about that back room was dead as well. And my sense from the evidence is that Sanderson got rid of them that last night."

"So we're going back into the tunnel?" Sarge asked.

Pickett nodded. "From the hotel side."

Sarge just shook his head. "Lovely, just lovely."

"I'll call the hotel manager," Robin said. "Get that set up. You thinking an hour?"

Pickett nodded. "If I can get The Cowboy here by then."

"I'll call Heidi at the historical society," Sarge said. "You know, crawling around underground looking for bodies has stopped being fun."

Pickett just laughed. "Can't remember when it ever was."

Both of them nodded to that.

CHAPTER TWENTY-SIX

January 30th, 2023
Las Vegas, NV

Sarge knew the missing musicians wasn't really their case if a case at all. Nowhere could they find missing person's reports filed on anyone that might have worked at the speakeasy in 1933 when it shut down.

But those instruments just left like that haunted him and a couple times he had even dreamed about them. The dreams would make a great Twilight Zone episode with the ghosts of the musicians getting back together for one last night playing in that old speakeasy.

He was glad he had been wrong about the bodies in the hidden rooms, but now Pickett's theory that the bodies were behind the doors in the tunnel made sense. Too much sense, actually. From the sounds of what Sanderson was like, he would never leave other people alive that knew about that money.

Sarge told Heidi what they were doing and she wanted to go along, even though she was not excited at all that they were once again looking for bodies. Sarge agreed with that. No one was excited about this trip into that old tunnel.

So one hour after Sarge left a second dessert unfinished in the buffet, he and Pickett and Robin met The Cowboy, Heidi, and Baker in the back of the Golden Nugget casino and started through a door and down some stairs.

Three minutes later they were standing in front of an area where blocks had been taken out of a basement wall exposing a wooden door on a wall on the other side.

The door and the hole in the basement wall had been taped off with crime scene and bright yellow warning tape.

The Cowboy handed Pickett and Sarge and Heidi helmets with lights on them. Then handed Pickett one radio and Robin the other. Robin and Baker were going to stay by the door and be ready to call for help if something went wrong.

Baker handed the four of them oxygen masks. And both Sarge and Pickett had crime scene gloves for everyone. Sarge and The Cowboy also carried a crowbar and hammers to pry open the doors if they needed to.

Heidi touched Baker's arm before she turned and stepped through the tape as Pickett pulled it aside. Sarge just smiled. Good to see two people with the same interests making a go of it. Especially as nice and driven as both of them were.

No one said anything as The Cowboy led the way down the tiled staircase. Heidi followed him and then Pickett with Sarge being last. All of them had seen this before. In fact, Heidi had been on this staircase a great deal, taking pictures of everything, including the old Otis elevator off to one side. Clearly the oldest elevator in Las Vegas. Kind of felt right it being under the oldest hotel still standing in Las Vegas.

The Cowboy studied the structure of the narrow brick tunnel even more carefully than the first time before they headed through it and into the larger tunnel.

"Safe?" Pickett asked him.

"Safe enough," The Cowboy said.

Sarge didn't much like that answer. Especially fifty feet under the street.

"Want to start with the closest door?" the Cowboy asked.

"If we're going to find bodies," Pickett said, "I'm betting they are behind the door under Las Vegas Boulevard."

Sarge agreed and down the tunnel they went, following The Cowboy.

They again stayed in single file and followed their own tracks. Sarge was surprised at how slanted the tunnel was. He hadn't noticed that the first time. But this time it clearly felt like they were going deeper underground, even though they were just following the slant of the surface road five stories above them.

They passed the other two doors quickly and it didn't take long at all to reach the door under Las Vegas Blvd.

They all stopped and just faced it, the lights from their helmets bringing out every detail in the rough wood of the door and the tunnel siding.

Then Sarge noticed something in the bright light of the four helmets. There were dark stains on the wood of the door and dark dots of stain covering the wood slats and on the beams to the side of the door.

"Blood stains and splatter," he said, pointing out what he was seeing. Over the years he had seen that so much that even after ninety years of fading he still recognized it.

"Damn it," Pickett said. "I so wanted to be wrong about this."

Pickett took the radio and said to Robin. "Call an active detective and a forensic team. We're at the door under Las Vegas Boulevard and we have clear blood stains and splatter."

"If this had been out in the weather," Sarge said, studying some of the stains closer, "they would have long ago vanished."

"Amazing what being underground preserves," The Cowboy said.

"Does that mean there will be bodies behind that door?" Heidi asked, her breathing clearly faster.

"Just means something happened at this spot a long time ago," Sarge said.

"And no footprints in the dust leading to the door," Pickett said, "so clearly this happened back when the tunnel was being used."

"Got something else," The Cowboy said.

He was pointing up near one of the old lights on top of one of the large beams.

It took Sarge a second to see it, but when he did he was amazed they had walked under that beam twice. Guns.

"Looks like two pistols and a shotgun," The Cowboy said.

Pickett called Robin again. "We have old guns as well."

"Well damn it all to hell," Robin said.

Sarge just laughed. He felt the same exact way. He turned to the wooden door. He now had little doubt what they were going to find back there. The body of everyone who had known the location of the money.

He did not want to open that door, but it seemed they had no choice now.

CHAPTER TWENTY-SEVEN

January 30th, 2023
Las Vegas, NV

Pickett looked at Sarge and he nodded.

"Masks, everyone," Pickett said and then put on hers, letting her ears adjust for the moment to the sound of her own breathing.

"Heidi," Sarge said, "you and The Cowboy stand back. No point in you seeing this."

"Like hell," The Cowboy said, stepping forward, his voice muffled only slightly by the mask. "Not letting either one of you open that door or go into that tunnel without me checking every bit of it first. A guy who could gun down people could just as easily have set a trap for anyone looking for his victims."

Pickett just stared at The Cowboy and then nodded. He was right, of course.

The Cowboy stepped up to the door and inspected it all the way around, then nodded to Sarge.

"Open it real slowly only about an inch or so."

Sarge nodded and took hold of the handle on the lower side. Even though he had gloves on, Pickett knew Sarge did that to not smudge any fingerprints that might be on the handle.

The door seemed to stick for a moment, then eased open.

Sarge stepped out of the way to let The Cowboy inspect it carefully.

"Seems clear, but open it slowly."

Sarge again nodded and did as The Cowboy said.

Pickett's light hit what was on the floor inside the door before Sarge and The Cowboy's lights did.

Six men's bodies, all mummified, sitting with their backs to the tunnel walls, three on one side, three on the other.

All seemed to be staring straight ahead with big empty eye sockets. Amazing what deep underground and dry desert conditions could do to a body.

All the men were dressed in dark suits from the 1930s and all clearly had gunshot wounds of one type or another. Two had been hit with shotgun blasts.

"Found the band," Sarge said softly, barely loud enough for Pickett to hear over her mask.

Pickett called Robin. "Six bodies. Mummified, more than likely from 1933."

"Copy that," Robin said. "Actives and forensic team on the way."

"How is the tunnel for the forensic team to work in here?" Pickett asked The Cowboy.

"Solid," he said. "Not vouching for what is beyond the bodies."

Sarge glanced at Pickett and she knew exactly what he was thinking.

"We need to check out the rest of the tunnel," Sarge said. "See where it ends."

The Cowboy nodded.

Pickett just hoped there were no more bodies.

CHAPTER TWENTY-EIGHT

January 30th*, 2023*
Las Vegas, NV

The way the bodies were seated, Sarge knew there was enough room to get by them without touching anything or disturbing any evidence.

Sarge glanced around. Heidi was standing in the door, staring at the six mummified men sitting against the walls.

"You can wait in the tunnel," Pickett said to her.

"Not a chance in hell," she said.

Pickett nodded and Sarge laughed softly. He would not have wanted to wait alone in that tunnel with six dead men that close.

The Cowboy, followed by Sarge, picked his way past the bodies.

"Stay with me," Pickett said to Heidi, "and don't look at them."

"Oh, trust me," Heidi said, "I will be seeing them in my nightmares for years."

Sarge actually knew he wouldn't be seeing these six. It was the five around the table in the speakeasy that would haunt him. At least until they found out who killed them and why.

It was clear who killed these six. More than likely it was Sanderson to protect his stash of money. Little good it did him.

The tunnel turned slightly to the right in about fifty steps, then opened up into a larger round room, all tiled with black and white tiles on the floor like the speakeasy and concrete walls with huge beams for the ceiling.

"What in the world is this for?" Pickett asked.

They all stopped and gave The Cowboy time to inspect it all.

"It's solid," he said after a long moment.

"What is this place?" Heidi asked. "Clearly built about the same time as the speakeasy and the Independence."

Pickett looked around. None of this made any sense.

There were five wooden doors spaced evenly leading from the round room on the opposite side that they had come in. The light from their helmets made it look even brighter than it had likely been from the one chandelier in the middle of the room.

"Door number one, two, three, four, or five?" Sarge asked.

Pickett just shook her head as The Cowboy went to inspect the first door on the left.

"Pickett," Robin said over the radio. "Actives and forensic team are here."

"We're exploring the tunnel beyond the bodies," Pickett said. "Making sure it is safe."

"I'll tell them," Robin said.

The Cowboy gave the okay and Sarge carefully pulled open the door on the left.

The Cowboy shined his light inside to make sure it was safe, then said simply, "Now I am officially having nightmares about this."

Sarge could only agree. On the other side of the door was what looked like a fully furnished 1930s hotel room.

And another mummy in the bed. A woman dressed in what looked like party clothes from the 1930s.

The top of her head had been destroyed by a shot.

CHAPTER TWENTY-NINE

January 30th, 2023
Las Vegas, NV

Pickett radioed Robin. "Got another body."

"Coming down with the actives," Robin said. "They both want you to just stop it."

"Wait until you see this one," Pickett said.

The Cowboy was right. This was the stuff of nightmares.

But thankfully the other four rooms looked almost identical to the first one, but no bodies.

Heidi and Pickett explored the hotel-sized area of the middle door the lamps on their helmets casting strange shadows everywhere. The bed filled the center of the room with an overstuffed fainting couch pushed against one wall. There were a couple of chairs, a very small round table, some booze and glasses on a nightstand. Just not much else at all.

Pickett glanced around at Heidi, who was seemingly doing well even with all the bodies. She was inspecting the bed without touching it or its metal frame, or the blankets on top of it. It had been expertly made almost 90 years ago. Just amazing.

"Any idea what all this was for?" Pickett asked.

"Working women," Heidi said without hesitation. "They would more than likely find a man with money and too much to drink in the speakeasy, bring him down here, and then escort him to the stairs under the hotel before going back to work."

"More than likely Sanderson got a cut of it all?" Pickett asked.

"Closer to all of it," Heidi said. "Normal for the times. But no idea why the one woman was killed, though. The working women would have never had access to behind the bar or the back rooms."

"Wrong place, wrong time," Pickett said.

Heidi nodded. "More than likely."

Twenty minutes later Pickett and Sarge were headed back to the hotel staircase with The Cowboy and Heidi. The case was active and they were done.

Two hours later Pickett and Sarge were having a wonderful steak dinner at the steakhouse on top of Binion's after showering and changing clothes.

Not once during the steak dinner, two glasses of wine, and fresh cheesecake for dessert did the case come up.

Not once.

And Pickett didn't even realize that until she and Sarge were cuddling on the couch with a fresh batch of popcorn and a hoped-for good movie.

And then it was only a fleeting thought. It was no longer their case once again. They were retired, what they had found was an active murder scene. And she doubted the bodies they had found today would ever be cold cases.

Sanderson had killed them to protect his money, she was sure of that. Open and shut.

Not like the five in the speakeasy.

Those were cold cases and getting colder by the day.

But tonight, with the man she loved and a good movie, she didn't plan on giving them a thought.

Tomorrow would be soon enough.

Part Five

ASK WHY?

CHAPTER THIRTY

January 31st, 2023
Las Vegas, NV

Sarge and Pickett had walked the five blocks to the Main Street Station buffet to meet Robin for breakfast. The day had started off bright blue and clear sky, but there was a solid wind out of the west, coming off the snow-covered mountains above the valley, so it was a cold winter's walk.

Surprisingly cold as far as Sarge was concerned.

Very, very few tourists were in sight, and those that were must have been warned about the cold because they all wore heavy ski parkas.

Sarge seldom wore gloves and a hat, but this morning he wished he had. His ears were actually aching when they finally got to the buffet. And they had walked at a faster pace than their normal stroll. He was glad for that as well.

Sarge had managed to put the bodies they had found yesterday out of his mind for the most part. He was just glad the mystery of what happened to the band had been solved. And it was one thing to see a mummified body over ninety years dead. Very different impact than a body still warm and covered in blood.

Robin was again ahead of them and already eating at their favorite table. They dropped their coats with only a good morning and rounded up food. Sarge did his normal different helpings of meat, including this morning some freshly sliced ham that looked great.

"Any news," Pickett asked as they returned to the table, fresh cups of coffee steaming in front of their places.

"Actives have identities of all of the bodies except the woman in the bed," Robin said. "Chances are they will never figure out her name. But the others were all reported missing at one point or another that year, five of them were musicians."

Sarge nodded. He had no doubt that was what had happened to them.

Robin went on. "The detectives on this are in agreement with our theory that Horace Sanderson did all this to protect his hidden money. Guns were his and they were the murder weapons."

"How in the world did they know they were his guns?"

Robin smiled. "Vegas for a long time required anyone entering town to check in their guns. At one point Sanderson had checked all three guns we found in the tunnel in with the sheriff. But he had checked them out at one point when he left town and never checked them back in when he got back."

"The old gun laws of the West win again," Pickett said, laughing.

Sarge just shook his head. No doubt who killed those seven and who left all the money in that hidden room. The 1933 murders were solved. The 1971 murders were a completely different question.

They talked and ate for a time and then all three of them went back for desserts. As Sarge was working on a pretty good piece of peach pie, Pickett spoke up.

"We still have to figure out who the woman was that killed Becky Williams, Kevin Donnally, Katie Stevens, Rusty Buhl, and Connie Carlson."

"And why she did it?" Sarge said.

Robin and Pickett both nodded, but neither said a word, which didn't bode well for them making any more progress on the case because he honestly had no ideas either.

Not a one.

CHAPTER THIRTY-ONE

January 31st, 2023
Las Vegas, NV

Pickett sat staring at the remains of her apple pie. It had tasted good a moment before, but now it seemed as bland as she was feeling without a lead in the case they had been assigned.

They had solved Becky Williams's missing person case, but were a long, long way away from figuring out who had killed her. Let alone why.

"Well," Robin said, "we know our killer wore size six shoes."

"Size six?" Pickett asked.

Robin studied the report again and then nodded. "Could not tell the brand, but they were fairly new shoes and size six."

"Wow, that's small," Pickett said.

"By modern standards, yes," Robin said. "But this was fifty-plus years ago. Women's feet in this country have gotten larger over the last three decades, so this wasn't that unusual."

"What size do you wear?" Sarge asked Pickett.

"Eight," she said.

"So would the size of the killer's shoe indicate how tall and heavy she might have been?" Sarge asked.

Robin again nodded. "The lab puts her at about five feet four inches and light, and it says here she was more than likely wearing a tight skirt of the fashion of the time because of the restrictive nature of her stride."

Pickett laughed. "Well, that's more than we had."

"Which was nothing," Sarge said, pushing the remains of his peach pie away. "But how about we focus on who might have known about that speakeasy in 1971."

"Too many," Robin said. "Anyone who visited it through that tunnel in the years it was open. Thirty-eight years later, many of them would have still been alive and maybe telling their kids or grandkids about it."

Pickett nodded. "But with Sanderson killing all his employees to guard the money and then him dying, the place faded into legend fairly quickly. More than likely all doors to it locked up tight."

Sarge nodded. "And with the casino changing hands a few times, no reason for anyone to go into that sub-basement."

"Except Miss Size Six and her companions," Robin said.

Sarge only nodded to that.

"But," Pickett said, "Las Vegas legends always take press to be remembered and maintained, such as newspaper articles and books. Who wrote about the times and such of the Independence speakeasy in the early 1970s?"

Robin looked at Pickett for a moment, then grabbed her phone. "I'll get my research people on it. You call Heidi."

"You think there might be an expert on the place through the years?" Sarge asked.

Robin shrugged. "There might be. A better chance than Miss Size Six buys us."

Pickett could only agree with that as she waited for Heidi to answer.

CHAPTER THIRTY-TWO

January 31st, 2023
Las Vegas, NV

Sarge went back for another piece of peach pie as both Robin and Pickett talked on their phones. When he got back they were both finished.

"My researchers tell me it will only be ten to fifteen minutes for them to do a good, solid basic scan of articles and books mentioning the speakeasy in that late 1960s and early 1970s timespan."

"Heidi says she remembers a couple of books and will be back with me shortly with what she finds as well," Pickett said.

"So we thinking a book or an article might be a link to tie the six together?" Sarge asked.

"I would call this grasping for straws," Pickett said, "but all we need is one straw."

Sarge could only agree. At this point any straw would be grand.

Two minutes later Robin's phone rang and she nodded, wrote something down on the file in front of her, and said, "Thanks," before hanging up.

"One major book on the speakeasy places in Las Vegas," Robin said, "published in early 1972."

At that moment Pickett's phone rang. She put it on speaker and said, "Thanks, Heidi. You have me and Robin and Sarge on speaker."

"One major book called *Las Vegas Underground* published in early 1972 detailing out all the establishments that were known to have existed in Prohibition."

Robin nodded and pointed to the note she had written down confirming it was the same book.

"The author's name was C. M. Carlson. Short for Connie Carlson, one of the women at the death table. It was published eight months after she disappeared and has been out of print since 1974."

Sarge just sat back, stunned. How in the world could this be?

Pickett was staring at the phone shaking her head.

"It wasn't until you called and asked about reference books that I finally put it together."

"What did she say about the place?" Sarge asked.

"She said it had been destroyed and turned into a laundry and furnace room in the remodeling for the apartments."

"So that's where that rumor started," Robin said, shaking her head as well.

"We have a copy in our library," Heidi said, "and I am sending you all a picture we just scanned from the book."

A moment later Sarge got the image on his phone and opened it.

A very clear picture of the main room and bar of the speakeasy.

"Take a close look at the image," Heidi said. "You can see the slight dust on everything."

And then Sarge saw it. In the reflection of the mirror behind the bar, there were six chairs pulled away from one table and bottles on the table and empty glasses, not yet filled.

The death scene, before those five drank the poison.

No one was in the picture. They must have been standing off to one side out of the reflection of the mirrors.

"Holy shit!" Pickett said.

"That picture was in the book published eight months after they all died down there," Heidi said. "It is labeled '1930s image of the Independence speakeasy.'"

"It seems we have a lead on Miss Size Six," Sarge said after a long silence.

But after fifty years, he didn't give the lead much hope at all, but at least it was a lead.

CHAPTER THIRTY-THREE

January 31st, 2023
Las Vegas, NV

Pickett gave Heidi directions on whom to get the book to at police headquarters and then hung up. That image needed to be studied by experts for any more clues.

Pickett stared at the image on her phone. It felt like something right out of a horror movie. The chairs pulled back, the bottles and glasses on the table. She could still see clearly in her mind those five mummified bodies in those chairs.

Damn creepy picture taken just minutes before five murders.

Robin was on the phone with her research people, trying to get information about the publishing house and Connie Carlson and her family.

Sarge was just sitting back in his chair staring at his phone.

"You all right?" she asked him.

"Just damn puzzled is all," he said. "That picture somehow got taken by Miss Size Six out of that death scene, and in the book to be published, the description of the speakeasy was changed to hide its true existence, and then the picture inserted. So first off, who could do that to Connie Carlson's book?"

Pickett nodded to that question.

"But what has me the most puzzled is why," Sarge said. "Clearly Miss Size Six wanted to keep the place hidden as much as Sanderson had back thirty-eight years before. Why?"

"I got a hunch we answer that question," Pickett said, "we find our killer."

At that moment Robin hung up and glanced at her notes before turning to them.

"Publisher of the book is long out of business," Robin said. "It was a regional press that specialized in publishing books about the Southwest. My people are trying to find out what happened to all of their files and such and find anyone who worked for them in 1971 who might still be alive."

Pickett nodded to that. "We might be able to find out who turned in the book for Carlson, or if it was turned in, who altered it."

Robin nodded.

"What about Carlson's family?" Sarge asked.

"Parents both dead, but a younger brother I mentioned earlier is still alive and weirdly enough he retired here in Vegas."

"Might be worth a conversation to see what he remembers about that book getting turned in," Sarge said.

"I agree," Pickett said. "And he might remember some of his sister's friends at the time."

"What exactly do we know about her?" Sarge asked.

"Not much at all," Robin said. "She had a masters in history and minored in English and loved the Southwest. This was her first and only book. Nothing besides that. Not even a picture."

"So we go talk with the brother," Sarge said. "Got his number by any chance?"

Robin nodded and gave Sarge the number and address of a home out in Summerlin.

For the first time since they found the bodies, Pickett felt a slight bit of hope that they might get a lead or two on the killer. Slight, but a lot better than she had been so far.

CHAPTER THIRTY-FOUR

January 31st, 2023
Las Vegas, NV

Sarge pulled his Cadillac SUV up in front of the two-story brown stucco home in Summerlin and let it run to keep the heat on. Even with the sun, the late morning was still bitterly cold, as only the desert could get cold with its dry air and almost constant wind.

And Summerlin was one of those planned developments that sat on the side of the hill overlooking Vegas, with almost every house with a view of the Strip in the distance. Clearly this home, that looked almost exactly like every other home along the street, was no exception to the view rule.

Sarge always wondered how people found their own homes in developments like this one. With the garage doors all closed, five houses in a row all looked identical. Only differences were the big black numbers on the side of the garage.

Connie Carlson's brother, Ed Carlson, said he would be happy to talk with them about Connie so they agreed to meet at eleven. It took Sarge and Pickett time to walk back to their condo, grab the car keys and make the thirty-minute drive up onto the hill.

They barely made it in time.

Sarge finally nodded to Pickett. "First interview since before the pandemic."

She laughed. "After all the decades of doing them, I don't think we have forgotten how."

So a moment later, their coats wrapped tight around them against the chill of the wind off the snow on the mountains above them, they rang the bell.

A long minute later, although Sarge guessed it was only twenty or thirty seconds, but it felt like a minute because of the cold, Ed answered the door and invited them in.

They introduced themselves as they entered and he seemed genuinely happy to meet them.

Carlson looked like he could lose a good hundred pounds, but clearly in his early days he had been lifting a lot since his shoulders were huge and he had very little neck, as if he had played football. He did have a wide grin full of perfectly white teeth and a deep voice that made it possible that with a beard he could play Santa during the holidays.

He was dressed in the standard Vegas golf clothes. Tan slacks, a white golf shirt under a tan button-down golf sweater. Sarge had no doubt there was a golf cart in the garage that he could drive to a nearby course most days of the week.

Thankfully, Carlson kept his big place very warm and they went past the brown and tan living room furniture that did not look used to a glass kitchen table. Sarge had been right about the views. Out a large patio door the Vegas Strip sat like toy buildings in the center of the valley below.

Carlson offered them both coffee and they both accepted as they slipped out of their winter coats, and then after he served them, he took a cup himself and sat across from them.

"Are you the two detectives who found my sister's body?"

"We are," Sarge said.

"Thank you," Carlson said. "I can't begin to tell you what a relief it was to finally know what happened and give her a proper burial in our family plot in Chicago."

Both Sarge and Pickett nodded. Not a lot they could say about that.

Then after a moment Pickett said, "We are still trying to figure out who did this."

"There is a chance of that after fifty years?" Carlson asked. "Amazing."

"Not a great chance," Sarge said, "but you could sure help us out if you can remember a few things about Connie."

"I'll try," Carlson said, nodding. He reached behind him and took a framed photo from the shelf. He handed it to Sarge, and Pickett leaned over to look.

The picture was of a young college guy in 1970s style jeans and a flannel shirt with a backpack on his shoulder and a young woman in a bright blue short skirt and white blouse. They were leaning into each other and both smiling, and they clearly looked alike.

"This is me and Connie the last time she was in Chicago and the last time I saw her. She had just turned twenty-three."

"Great memory," Sarge said, handing back the photo. He didn't know if it was good or bad that he now had an image of Connie in his mind.

"Did you know she was working on a book about speakeasies?" Pickett asked.

"Sure," Carlson said. "It started out as part of her master's thesis and just grew from there. We talked about it every week. In fact, she was home in Chicago when she got the call from her editor that the publisher had accepted her book."

Carlson laughed. "We might have celebrated a little too much that night." He smiled and clearly was lost in a very good memory.

Sarge gave him a moment before asking, "Any chance you might remember the editor's name?"

"Maggie something," Carlson said. "Connie was always talking about Maggie this and Maggie that. Seemed they had really hit it off and were becoming friends."

Sarge felt a slight surge of excitement with that information, but tamped it down and went on.

Pickett wrote the information in her notebook, nodding.

"Do you know if Connie was going out with anyone at the time of her disappearance?" Pickett asked.

"She told me the week before she vanished that she really liked a young golf pro," Carlson said. "I read in the paper that she was found with four others and one was a golf pro. More than likely that was him, but I have no memory of his name at all."

"Why do you think it might be him?" Sarge asked.

"Because when Connie vanished, I never got a call from any golf pro or any other boyfriend. Lots of her friends called me and asked if they could help look for her in San Diego. We just didn't know where to start looking to be honest. Had not realized she had come back here. More than likely to visit her publisher, who was based here from what I understand."

"Who turned in her book to the publisher?" Pickett asked.

Carlson just shrugged. "I just assumed it was turned in before she vanished. I got a couple copies of it here on the shelf if you want to see it."

"Thanks," Pickett said. "We have a copy as well."

Carlson just nodded.

"Did you get a call from the publisher asking where she was at?" Sarge asked.

"I did," Carlson said. "They even put up a reward of five thousand dollars for information. That was the same size as her advance, actually. A lot of money back in 1971."

Sarge nodded and they asked a few more questions, but nothing came of it. They left thirty minutes later after finishing their coffee and promising Carlson that they would keep him informed about any information they found.

Sarge felt great about what they had found.

At least it was something.

CHAPTER THIRTY-FIVE

February 1st, 2023
Las Vegas, NV

When they finished talking with Connie Carlson's brother, Robin said it was going to take time to track down the information they had found about the publishing company. It actually took until the next morning to track down anything about the publisher and his staff and the editor Maggie. Fifty-one years and lack of information being put into digital form can do that.

So after the interview with Ed, Pickett and Sarge had gone back to their condo, got take-out from a great Thai restaurant, and watched a forgettable movie. They didn't want to talk about the case until they had more information, so they just didn't.

One of the many things Pickett loved about their relationship and the incredible man she had fallen for.

As normal, the next morning they all met in the Main Street Station buffet just after nine. The walk had been cold, but Pickett didn't think it was as bad as the day before, since the wind had dropped. In fact, she kind of enjoyed the walk. But she always enjoyed being with Sarge, no matter what they were doing.

She just couldn't believe how lucky she had been finding him so late in both of their lives. They just fit together in so many ways.

When they got to the buffet, Robin had her laptop computer open and was intensely working on something on the laptop at their favorite table while eating. They both took off their coats without saying even good morning to her, went and got food, and came back.

"Found the publisher," Robin said as they put their plates on the table and settled in. "Lost Nevada Press was the company name. They published the book under the imprint Hidden History Press."

Pickett just smiled. In all the years they had been partners on the force, Robin had always been that driven and focused. Pickett couldn't begin to count the number of lunches they had eaten together with Robin buried in her computer or making calls.

"Publisher still alive?" Sarge asked.

"He is," Robin nodded, "and is willing to talk with us. He lives here in Vegas in the Henderson area. Name is Stephen Black and he is seventy-eight years old."

"Wow," Pickett said, surprised. "He was young when he was a publisher."

"Trust fund money, but not enough," Robin said. "The company only lasted four years and published six books total, one of which was Connie's book. Black ended up in advertising and had his own agency until he retired a decade or so ago."

Pickett nodded. The two jobs sort of fit together.

"He's expecting you two at eleven a.m.," Robin said, sliding Pickett the address and phone number on a slip of paper.

"Fun having something to do on this case," Sarge said.

"You mean other than finding a hidden speakeasy?" Pickett asked, trying not to laugh.

Robin did laugh. "Don't forget exploring a tunnel under the town and finding twelve bodies?"

Sarge just shook his head. "Yeah, besides that."

Pickett touched his hand and the three of them went back to eating. Pickett knew how he was feeling. They knew who had killed the seven in 1933, to protect the secret of the money. But no idea besides a shoe size who had killed the five in 1971. And even what those six people were all doing down there together.

Suddenly Pickett had a thought. "Could the money be what is tying all this together?"

Sarge and Robin both looked up at her with puzzled expressions.

"Do we know how much money was in that secret room?"

Robin pulled a report out of her computer bag and opened it. A moment later she said, "Just over six million. All in 1933 and before bills. So a lot of it is collectable as well."

"Wow," Sarge said. "How much would that be in 1971 money value?"

Robin did a quick calculation on her computer. "That six million in 1971 would be worth about forty-five million today if it had been invested.

Robin just shook her head, staring at the number on the screen. "Six million sure went a lot farther in 1971."

Pickett looked at Sarge, then at Robin. "So in 1971 could anyone have known that money was there? Maybe Miss Size Six?"

"If so," Sarge said, "just like with Sanderson, none of the money was touched. Why not?"

"Great," Pickett said. "Another mystery to add to the pile of this twisted mess."

CHAPTER THIRTY-SIX

February 1st, 2023
Las Vegas, NV

Sarge pulled up his Cadillac SUV in front of a single-story ranch house that looked like it had been built back in the 1960s. Vegas had a lot of very deceptive homes like this one in the high-end older subdivisions. They looked like regular old ranch homes from the front, but would often have five or six bedrooms, a massive master suite, and a guest house beside the pool out back. This house looked like it might be one of those hidden monsters and the neighborhood and the house were all beautifully kept up.

And if Black had his own ad agency, more than likely this house was worth a bunch of money, especially in this classic upscale neighborhood.

Black opened the big wooden front door for them before they were halfway up the sidewalk between rocks and desert landscaping. Grass in homes in Las Vegas had mostly been replaced with low-water shrubs and plants over the last decade to save water and money.

Black was tall and thin, with a long receding hairline and long silver-white hair. His clothes were very expensive brown dress slacks and what looked to be a silk dress shirt. He stood ramrod straight like he had been former military. The only sign of his age was an ornate walking stick in his right hand.

Sarge bet Black had always been tall and thin and in shape. He had that look about him. Sarge bet it was golf or tennis that kept Black in shape now. More than likely tennis.

Black gave them a wide smile of perfect white teeth and held the door open for them to come in.

It was a pretty standard living room of a ranch house, only with expensive white tile on the floor and very expensive white and brown furniture.

Pickett and Sarge introduced themselves and showed their badges and he nodded that they should all sit at an ornate dining room table to one side of the living room.

The art on the walls around the table all looked original and more than likely one piece cost more than Pickett and Sarge's penthouse condos combined.

A moment later a young woman, about college age, with a brown apron and long black hair came in and asked if they would like anything to drink. All three of them ordered coffee.

"So, detectives," Black said as she left, "I've been following in the papers the discovery of Connie Carlson in an old speakeasy under the Independence. Just amazing."

"Why amazing?" Pickett said a half second before Sarge could ask the same question.

"I remember she was so certain that the speakeasy was still there, but just couldn't prove it. She and Maggie, her editor, talked about it all the time. As the book neared press time and in the final copyedits, they went with the story that it had been destroyed in the remodeling. But Connie had another version of that chapter they could swap out at the last minute if she found proof."

"That is amazing," Sarge said, nodding.

"Any idea why anyone would want to kill her and the others down there?" Black asked.

"That's what we are trying to find out," Sarge said. "The why and the who."

Black just shook his head. "Not a bit of it makes sense."

Pickett laughed. "You have that right."

The coffee arrived on individual trays to protect the table and they all stopped to sip the coffee, a brand and brew Sarge had never tasted before, but wouldn't mind tasting again. It was some sort of dark roast with a slight hint of orange.

"So how can I help you, detectives?"

"Would you happen to have a list of all your publishing company employees that might have known Connie?"

Black just laughed. "There were only four of us. I was the publisher and money person. Andres Johnson was our layout and copyediting. Benny Wall was our sales. And Maggie Jay was our editor. She knew Connie very well, the others only talked with Connie in meetings. I shut everything down when Andres died suddenly in a skiing accident at Big Bear."

"So what happened to the other two?" Pickett asked.

"Benny and I went into advertising and Maggie married a childhood sweetheart she met up with again at a reunion. She worked as editor on a local paper for a time and now is retired after her husband died and is writing books from what I understand. Mystery thrillers."

"You know her married name?" Pickett asked.

Black took out his iPhone from his pocket and looked up the number. "Maggie Orchid. Lives out in a new development in North Las Vegas."

He gave Pickett the number and address to write down.

So they sipped their coffee for a moment before Sarge had a thought. "Any chance you might have some of the old records left from your publishing business?"

Black really laughed, deep and real. "I stupidly still have them all."

"You're kidding?" Pickett asked.

Black just laughed again. "You know I was young and worried about taxes, even though that press never came close to earning a nickel in profit. So I boxed everything up, every scrap of paper from everyone's office when I shut it down, and stored it all in the attic area of the garage out back here."

"You've owned this house the entire time?" Sarge said.

Black nodded. "A lot of remodeling and adding onto over the years, but never touched the old garage and you know, the idea of getting rid of all those boxes just never seemed to rise to the top of the priority list. And since I never moved, never had to deal with them. So everything is all there. But sure can't imagine how any of it would be worthwhile."

"Well," Sarge said, "on a case fifty-one years cold, all we can do is grasp at straws."

"Or thirty or forty boxes of straws," Black said, laughing. "Tell you what, you move and recycle the entire mess when you are through, you can have it all."

"We'll have young humans and a moving truck here tomorrow morning, if that works for you," Sarge said, sticking out his hand.

"Eleven a.m.," Black said, laughing and shaking Sarge's hand. "Just glad I don't have to move them."

"Oh, no worry," Sarge said. "We won't move them either. I'm years past moving boxes. But we will look through all of them between here and recycling."

"And if we find anything we think you might want to keep," Pickett said, "we'll call you."

"Thanks, but can't imagine what it might be," Black said. "But if you find that straw, do let me know."

CHAPTER THIRTY-SEVEN

February 2nd, 2023
Las Vegas, NV

Pickett suggested that they use her living room in her condo, since they mostly used Sarge's side of things after they had combined the two, and Sarge agreed.

Four very young and very strong movers made short work of the forty-odd filing boxes from Black's garage attic, dusting them and wiping them off as they loaded them into a large truck.

Then it didn't take much longer to get the boxes on handcarts up the elevator at the Ogden and placed on a large tarp in the middle of Pickett's living room.

The young movers had also moved Pickett's tan and brown furniture out of the way and covered it all as well to protect it. Then the movers placed another tarp on the tile floor to put the boxes designated for recycling.

As a final step, they moved Pickett's glass dining room table and three chairs down beside the pile of boxes so that Pickett and Sarge and Robin could sit and sort through boxes without moving them more than a few feet.

Sarge had the movers lined up to come back and take out the boxes to recycling and put all the furniture back as soon as he called them that the project was done.

Pickett had a hunch that even though the pile looked large, larger than she had expected actually, it would not take the three of them that long to search through the boxes looking for anything that might help.

All of them were still convinced that Connie's book had something to do with this. They just didn't know how.

Or worse, why.

And, of course, if they were wrong in thinking Connie's book had something to do with the murders, they would be back at the starting point again without even the slightest theory.

Robin stood near the table and stared out past the large pile over the downtown Las Vegas area and the Strip beyond. It was a stunningly blue and clear winter day and everything looked extra bright. "Got to say this might be the best view of any workroom I have ever seen."

Pickett glanced out the window. She had to admit that Robin was right and living here, she never got used to the view. She noticed it every day.

She had been lucky to have family money to have been able to afford this back before she met Sarge. Many nights, after a long day, she would just sit with a glass of wine and her feet up staring at the lights of the city. Amazingly calming.

Sarge clicked off his phone and put it back in his pocket as he stepped toward were Robin and Pickett were standing near the glass dining room table.

"Pizza will be here in about thirty minutes," he said. "Shall we get started?"

"Any idea what we might be looking for?" Robin asked, staring at the pile of old and yellowed file boxes and shaking her head.

"Not a clue," Pickett said. "But I think we'll know it if we see it."

"I would say we watch the dates as well," Sarge said. "Anything to do with Connie's book or anything else in the time ahead of the crime."

Pickett nodded. She agreed with that.

So Pickett took one box and put it beside the chair at the head of the table and tossed the lid aside as she sat down.

Robin did the same at the other end of the table with a box off the other side of the pile.

Sarge got a third box and sat in the middle of the table.

Pickett just shook her head as she grabbed the first folders full of receipts from back in the days before computers. They really were looking for any straw they could find.

And she wasn't honestly sure she would recognize it if she saw it.

CHAPTER THIRTY-EIGHT

February 2nd, 2023
Las Vegas, NV

They had found nothing in three hours after eating the pizza for lunch and the recycle pile of file boxes had grown larger than the pile they had left to go through. Sarge had to admit that Black had been very organized in his small publishing company. Very.

Sarge was about to suggest they break for dinner when Pickett said, "Take a look at this."

Both Sarge and Robin moved to stand behind Pickett.

"It seems that Maggie was working on a book from an author by the name of Adin Harrison at the same time she was working with Connie."

"So," Robin said.

Pickett pointed to the title of the book and Sarge read it aloud. "*Hidden Treasures of Southern Nevada.*"

He looked at Robin, then at Pickett. "You think this Harrison had rumors in his book about the money in the speakeasy?"

Pickett shrugged. "But Maggie killed the book two months before Connie's book was published."

Robin immediately turned to her computer and Sarge grabbed his phone and called Black.

"Sorry to bother you," Sarge said, "but do you remember a book by the name of *Hidden Treasures of Southern Nevada* by Adin Harrison?"

"Sure do," Black said. "I thought the book had a lot of promise, but Maggie thought it was just too much rumor and speculation and I went with her judgment on it and we passed on the book."

"How was his reaction? Do you happen to remember?"

"Angry," Black said. "And I do remember it cost me some attorney fees because he threatened that if we used any information from his book, he would sue us. Since we figured his book was all speculation and myth, we just laughed, our attorney read the manuscript and laughed as well, and nothing ever came of it."

"Is a copy of the manuscript in these boxes?" Sarge asked.

"Should be," Black said. "Everything else is."

"That's true," Sarge said. "I have to admit you were very organized."

"You are not the first person to say that over the years," Black said.

Sarge thanked him and clicked off his phone just as Robin turned away from the computer.

"Adin Harrison is still alive, retired from forty years with the water district, and living in North Las Vegas."

Sarge nodded. "Black said the manuscript for Harrison's book should be here."

"What do you say we find it and take it to dinner with us," Pickett said.

It took them only twenty minutes to find it, and twenty minutes after that they were sitting in a back booth of their favorite Mexican restaurant just three blocks from their condo.

And all Sarge could think about was reading that book. He would bet anything there was a chapter on the hidden money in the speakeasy.

And he would have won that bet.

CHAPTER THIRTY-NINE

February 2nd, 2023
Las Vegas, NV

The wonderful rich smells of spicy Mexican food filled the restaurant around Pickett, flowing seemingly like a river every time the door into the kitchen behind them was opened. The music was low and there were less than a dozen people in the large place, so it was easy to talk.

They had divided up the thick manuscript into three parts and Pickett ended up with the chapter titled, "Lost Hoarded Profits." It was about the Independence speakeasy.

"Found it," she said.

Robin and Sarge put away their parts of the book, and Pickett read the first page and then handed it to Sarge.

The author, Adin Harrison, started off describing the history of the speakeasy and the owner Sanderson and what he and his family were like. From all the records they had found about Sanderson, the author had the description down pretty solid.

The author then went into general information about how speakeasies were cash businesses and that cash from a popular place like the Independence had never appeared in any accounts of Sanderson.

Pickett made a note to ask Robin about how the author could have found out that information from 1933 in 1970. Granted, it was the recession and so many banks had failed, no one in 1933 really trusted banks. But Pickett still wanted to know how that banking information might have been possible to track.

Then the author went on speculating that a large amount of money would have been hidden every night in a secret room in the speakeasy and that few besides Sanderson would know about the room or how to find it.

Then he talked about Sanderson's sudden death and how it was doubtful with the relationship between Sanderson and his family back East that any of the money would have been taken out.

The author then speculated that the money would have been found if the Independence speakeasy had been torn out in the construction of the apartments in 1970, and that would have made news, but there was no record of that sort of discovery then.

So in his conclusion, Adin Harrison believed that the speakeasy was still there, filled with cash.

Pickett passed the last page of the chapter over to Sarge who read it and passed it to Robin.

It was at that point that the steaming and fantastic-smelling plates of food arrived along with margaritas for each of them.

As the waiters left, Robin shook her head and said, "Stunningly good detective work on Harrison's part."

"He described it totally," Sarge said.

"Was it possible for him to track the banking information like he claimed?"

"Sure," Robin said after her first bite off a large enchilada covered with red salsa. "In 1970 the banking information from 1933 would have mostly been preserved in boxes like we are digging through. If he knew the right people in the banks descended from the 1933 banks, he could have gotten access to the old records."

"Sounds like a horrid amount of work," Sarge said.

Robin nodded. "It would have been."

"Makes me think the rest of this book is not so far into speculation," Pickett said. "Might be worth looking at with more modern methods."

"Solving cold cases not challenging enough for you?" Sarge asked, smiling. "Now you want to go treasure hunting?"

"Got to admit it was fun finding this treasure," Pickett said.

"If you ignore the seven bodies tied to that treasure," Sarge said.

"And maybe five more," Robin said.

"You two sure know how to take the fun out of possible treasure," Pickett said, laughing.

CHAPTER FORTY

February 3rd, 2023
Las Vegas, NV

After dinner, they had headed back to the Ogden to finish up the sorting. They found nothing else of importance at all, so Sarge had called Black to make sure it was all right if they recycled everything, then Sarge set up with the movers to come and get it all in the morning.

It didn't take long for the movers to have it all in their truck except for the manuscripts from Connie and paperwork around that book and the manuscript from Harrison and the paperwork with it. Two boxes they kept sitting on the glass table.

As soon as the movers left, Pickett and Sarge headed for the Main Street Station buffet for breakfast. As normal, Robin was already there in the back and working on her computer between bites.

This morning the buffet felt a little more empty than usual, and even with the winter sun coming through the high windows, it felt gray and kind of depressing.

Sarge wasn't sure why he felt that way. More than likely he was hoping for more from the pile of boxes from Black. Finding the book by

Harrison was more than they had before, but not much more. And he was honestly worrying about approaching Harrison.

So far the police had managed to keep the news of finding the money out of the public knowledge. And Sarge wasn't sure if they should tell Harrison. They knew the killer was a woman, but that didn't mean Harrison hadn't been involved. Money on that scale made for strange partnerships.

So over breakfast they talked and decided that interviewing Harrison would be a good plan, but not telling him that the treasure he had thought was there actually had been there.

Sarge called him and he was happy to talk with them. So around eleven he and Pickett pulled up in front of a 1960s style home in a deteriorating neighborhood in North Las Vegas.

At first glance it was clear that Harrison had not spent much money keeping up the house. It seemed his wife had left him about twenty years before and left him the house and an old Plymouth that was still sitting in the driveway.

Harrison had done nothing special with his life, worked a government job until retirement, and that was that. It seemed his treasure book has been his passion when he was young and he had done nothing since. Or that was what it looked like sitting in front of the single-level house a few years past needing another coat of light blue paint.

Harrison met them at the door and stepped back as he invited them in after they flashed their badges.

Harrison was rail thin, maybe six-three in height, and had white hair and a white beard. Sarge could instantly see bright intelligence in his eyes. And the moment Sarge got inside, he understood why.

Every wall of what would have been the living room was covered with maps of one sort or another. With pins stuck in the maps and pictures of people and places all around each map.

One couch of questionable quality sat against one wall under a couple maps with piles of folders on it, and a large recliner faced an even larger television tucked in a corner.

"Let's go in the kitchen," Harrison said, his voice sounding like a deep professor's voice that didn't fit the tall, thin frame. "I cleaned off the table so we could talk there."

He led them to the old metal table and three metal chairs and indicated they should sit. He didn't offer than water or coffee or anything and Sarge was actually glad of that considering the slight smell coming from the stove and sink area.

Sarge could see down the hall toward the bedrooms. The hall was covered with more maps and pins and pictures. Files were stacked along the wall under each map.

Treasure maps. And the research that went along with them. Sarge was sure of that.

"What can I do for you, detectives?" Harrison asked after they got set.

"We have gone through the files of Lost Nevada Press," Pickett said, "and found a copy of your book with the chapter talking about the Independence speakeasy."

"Are you the detectives who found the place?" he asked, sitting forward.

Sarge nodded. "We are."

"I want to thank you," Harrison said. "You finally allowed Kevin and Katie's families to have some closure."

"You knew them?" Sarge asked, shocked.

Pickett looked shocked as well.

Harrison nodded. "My wife went to high school with them up in Boise and we were at their wedding here."

"Any idea how they ended up down in the speakeasy?" Pickett asked.

Harrison shrugged. "They loved my research on the old place, and my wife Kathy was friends with Maggie at the press and the four of them went out to lunches with Connie a few times together."

"You were all friends back then?"

Harrison nodded. "We were. I had no idea why Kevin and Katie and Connie all just suddenly left." He laughed to himself. "At least not until you two found their bodies."

"Did your wife seem upset about their just vanishing as well?" Pickett asked.

Harrison just shrugged. "I was so busy at the time with the idea of a lost gold mine in the Red Rocks above Vegas, I wasn't paying much attention. I knew the speakeasy was there so it no longer interested me."

"There's a mine up there?" Sarge asked.

Harrison just shrugged. "I could never prove it or find it, but a lot of evidence seems to lead to it being there."

"So were you surprised about the discovery of the Independence speakeasy?" Pickett asked, smiling at Sarge.

"No, as I said, I knew it was there and that it hadn't been torn out," Harrison said. "Just never knew how to get into it. I am surprised you didn't find Sanderson's money."

"Historical society and the state have the place locked down and guarded," Pickett said. "And it is still a crime scene so no one allowed in."

Harrison nodded. "Makes sense, but when they find it, trust me, it will be a lot of money. By my research, that speakeasy was really pulling in the big bucks at the time. And that was 1933. No telling what that treasure would be worth now."

"So you think your two friends and Connie were after the money?" Sarge asked.

Harrison shook his head. "I doubt it. I bet they just wanted to prove they could find it."

"To help you?"

Harrison shrugged at that. "I love the research and the hunt for hidden stuff. Finding it is often a letdown."

CHAPTER FORTY-ONE

February 3rd, 2023
Las Vegas, NV

Pickett just sat there sort of stunned at how this interview had gone. Harrison was not at all what she had expected, yet after looking at his book from the 1970s, she should have expected this.

"Do you still have your research on the speakeasy and the treasure?" Pickett asked.

Harrison shrugged. "Sure, let me show you. Now that it has been found, I was thinking of taking it down anyway and making room for another project."

He stood and led them down the hall and into the first door on the right, which was a small bedroom with a small desk and chair, both covered in files. In one corner of the room was tacked up a map of 1933 downtown Las Vegas.

Harrison pointed to it. It showed in faded red the speakeasy under the hotel and then also a tunnel going up the middle of Fremont to the old hotel on the corner of Main and Fremont.

Pickett was shocked. That map and the files and pins on it looked like they had been there for decades, more than likely over fifty years.

"That is what I assumed it looked like," Harrison said. "Customers had to enter from a major hotel of the time and go underground, so the speakeasy would be a distance underground as well under the hotel. Sanderson spared no expense on the hotel, so I assume he spared no expense building the speakeasy either. Only way it would have worked in those late 1920s times staying hidden from the Feds."

"You pretty much got it all correct," Sarge said.

Pickett just nodded, amazed at the detail of the map and how close it was to what was really there.

"Love to see it and walk that tunnel someday," Harrison said, shaking his head. Then he began to pull out the tacks to take down the map.

Pickett and Sarge watched, Pickett not sure what to feel. This man's entire life and work had been to study and find hidden treasures. She really wanted to tell him about the money being found as well, but it was not her position to do that.

"Files are those on the floor," Harrison said, pointing to the ones stacked under where he had just taken down the map.

Sarge took one pile and handed it to Pickett, then took the second pile.

"I sure hope something in here will help you discover who did this to my friends."

"It might," Sarge said. "More than we had, that's for sure."

"Do you think we can talk with your ex-wife?"

Harrison shrugged, as he rolled up the map, grabbed a tube from behind the small desk and stuck the map in the tube and then handed it to Sarge.

"I doubt she'll be able to help you. Twenty years ago she was diagnosed with early onset Alzheimer's. We got a divorce so she could get the care she needed from the State. I see her every week but she never recognizes me anymore. But you never know what she will remember or not remember at any given moment, so I still talk to her like we used to talk about the different treasures and searches and research and sometimes she responds."

"She was a part of all this?" Sarge asked.

Pickett felt surprised as well. She just had assumed that this was Harrison's passion and it had driven his wife to leave him.

Harrison laughed. "She was far, far more into all this than I was when we started. She kept us organized and was the driving force behind me writing that book because she said it would have had no chance at all in that time period coming from a woman."

He smiled, his gaze clearly on the past. "We sure had some great times searching for lost treasures."

Pickett glanced at Sarge, then took a deep breath and asked, "How tall is your wife? Not now, but back when your friends went missing?"

Harrison frowned, then said, "My height, thin as me. Robust. Why?"

"Just following every lead is all," Sarge said. "Thank you for all this. We'll keep it in good shape and return it to you when we are finished."

"Thanks," Harrison said, leading them out of the small bedroom and toward the front door. "Sure hope it helps."

"Just knowing why Kevin and Katie were with Connie down there has helped a lot," Pickett said. "A connection we do not have."

"And let me know when you find the money," Harrison said. "I am certain it is there. Or if you want to try to talk with my wife."

Pickett just nodded.

"Thanks again," Sarge said.

And with their arms full of more old documents, they headed through the cold morning toward the car.

CHAPTER FORTY-TWO

February 3rd, 2023
Las Vegas, NV

Robin joined Sarge and Pickett as they took the files and map from Harrison back up to the glass table in their condo.

After they gave Robin all the details about the interview with Harrison, Sarge asked, "Do you think it might be worth our time to talk with Harrison's wife?"

Pickett shrugged.

Robin also shrugged. "I will see if I can find out how her disease is manifesting. She might be able to remember details and flashes of memories from the past. But only as a lead. Nothing that would hold up in any kind of court."

"Well," Pickett said, "Let's hope we don't end up needing to grasp at that straw."

Sarge could only agree with that. Then he said, "Am I the only one who is starting to think that editor Maggie is our prime suspect?"

"Seems to be the only suspect left standing," Pickett said. "But if she did kill them and we approach her wrong, we'll lose any chance of finding out what really happened."

"I did a deep dive on her," Robin said. "She is the right size for the shoe prints, and she has had a couple of health scares over the last few years, but nothing that looks like it might knock her out soon enough for a deathbed confession."

Suddenly Sarge had an idea.

"Correct me if I am wrong," Sarge said, "But the door into the staircase and elevator to go down to the tunnel was covered over by a wall at some point in the casino's history. The one we had to cut through. Right?"

Robin and Pickett both nodded.

"And at some point the rope for the counterweight to open the doors in the basement of Independence broke."

Again, both nodded.

"So," Sarge said, "when was that wall built?"

Robin opened up her laptop and her fingers seem to blur they were moving so fast.

"You thinking Maggie killed them all, then left and waited for the smell to clear before going back to look for the money?" Pickett asked.

Sarge nodded. "And then she couldn't get in because of the wall and the broken counterweight."

"How long do you think she waited?" Pickett asked.

"Long enough for the smell to clear, to make sure the money was safe, and that she would never get caught."

"So," Pickett said, "to make sure nothing led back to her if the bodies were found, she had to change the chapter in Connie's book and kill Harrison's book, which was more than likely the way they found the speakeasy in the first place."

"And then she had to just wait," Sarge said. "Make sure no one discovered the bodies."

"The casino basement was remodeled and that wall built to close off that old door just four months after the murders," Robin said.

"And I'm betting the counterweight rope broke," Sarge said, "after thirty-eight years of non-use when they let Becky into the speakeasy from the hotel."

"If Maggie did this and went back a year later to find the money,"

Pickett said, "she must have been angry beyond belief when there was no way in."

Sarge nodded. "That kind of money that close and no way she dared get to it without being found out as a murderer."

"So we are in agreement?" Robin asked. "We think the killer is Maggie."

Sarge just nodded. He no longer had any doubts at all. They had found the speakeasy and if Harrison's friends left there, Harrison would know, and Connie would want the chapter in her book, and more than likely Harrison would get his book published.

And the treasure would end up going to the owners of the Independence. Maggie wanted that money and the only way to protect it was to kill the others with her.

So looked like that stash of money had ended up causing all twelve deaths associated with that speakeasy and tunnel.

"How do we prove she did it?" Pickett asked. "We don't have enough evidence at all right now, that's for sure."

Sarge had no idea at all. They had no real hard evidence that led to Maggie besides a shoe print. And that could have belonged to a thousand women in Vegas in 1971.

Talk about frustrating. They had figured out who had killed those five people and there was not a darned thing they could do about it.

Just nothing.

CHAPTER FORTY-THREE

February 4th, 2023
Las Vegas, NV

After a quick search through Harrison's paperwork, and spreading his map out on the glass table, they had finally called it a day. Nothing in the old notes that would help them in the slightest.

Robin had gone home to her husband to cook dinner and Pickett and Sarge had gone out to a nice steak house, then watched a movie, talking only rarely about the case.

This morning, on the walk to meet Robin at the Main Street buffet, they walked in the cold morning air in silence. But she had to admit the nice dinner and movie last night and the fresh air this morning on the walk helped clear her head. She had no doubt they just needed to go directly at Maggie. After all the years, it was the only hope they had.

After they got their food and joined Robin at their normal table, Sarge said what Pickett had been thinking.

"We need to talk with Maggie."

Robin nodded. "I agree."

"Thinking the same way," Pickett said, surprised that all of them had come to the exact same conclusion.

They ate for a moment in silence. Pickett just didn't like the idea of going straight at a killer. But sometimes the direct approach saved a lot of time. If Maggie did it, maybe after over fifty years, she was ready to confess. And if she didn't do it, that meant a killer was still out there somewhere.

Robin slid a piece of paper to Pickett. "Maggie's address in North Las Vegas."

"Think we should just surprise her?" Sarge asked.

Pickett shook her head. "I think we should call her like we do all the others. We might be wrong about her after all."

"I agree," Sarge said.

Robin nodded and picked up her phone. When Maggie answered, Robin introduced herself and asked if Maggie would be willing to talk to a couple detectives about her former author Connie Carlson.

Robin listened for a moment, then nodded and said, "Wonderful. We'll be there at twelve."

"You going with us on this one, huh?" Pickett asked, smiling at her old friend and partner.

"Would not miss this for anything," Robin said. "And I will be wired up and recording the interview just in case."

Pickett nodded. "Really good plan."

"Really good," Sarge said. "I'm just glad you left us time to grab more dessert."

Pickett laughed. "Is dessert all you're think about?"

"Better than thinking about confronting a possible killer," he said standing to go get more dessert, "or the mummified bodies."

"He has a point," Robin said, pushing aside her mostly finished first plate and standing.

"I'll meet you both there," Robin said, also standing. "I'm heading home to get wired up and make sure one of our techs is recording everything."

"Really glad you are doing that," Pickett said.

Robin nodded and started toward the entrance. "Just have a piece of key lime pie for me."

"With pleasure," Pickett said. "With pleasure."

CHAPTER FORTY-FOUR

February 4th, 2023
Las Vegas, NV

Sarge pulled his Cadillac SUV in front of the address that Robin had given him and left the car running to keep himself and Pickett warm while they waited for Robin. The home was a fairly new suburban home with stucco siding and large windows with the blinds opened. It looked like three of the other houses on the street, just painted a slightly different color.

Sarge looked around and just shook his head. He would never understand subdivisions like this one.

"You worried about this?" Pickett asked.

"I am," Sarge said. "But not for the reason you might think. I'm more afraid she didn't do it and we will be back to square one."

"Yeah," Pickett said. "That worries me as well."

At that moment Robin pulled her Lexus sedan up behind Sarge's SUV and a moment later got out. Sarge shut off the car and he and Pickett both climbed out.

"Well," Robin said as they reached the sidewalk and started up toward the house between the rocks and cactus landscaping. "Here we go."

Maggie opened the door for them before Robin could knock.

Sarge was a little stunned. Maggie actually looked like an elderly woman much older than her age, bent over and using a walker. She was very short to start with and was made even shorter by the posture. She had on a housecoat-looking dress and slippers that made her look even older.

But her smile was wide with good teeth and her eyes were bright.

She held the door open with a shaking hand as Robin showed her badge and introduced the three of them.

Then Maggie said, "Come in. I just put on a fresh pot of coffee."

The interior of the home was as modern-looking as the outside, all furnished in tan furniture on white tile floors. Nothing at all looked out of place and it wasn't too warm or too cold.

Using her walker, Maggie led them fairly slowly to a table just off the kitchen and then turned for the kitchen.

"Can I help with that?" Pickett asked.

"That would be lovely," Maggie said. "I don't get around as well as I used to since my last stroke. But I'm still here." Maggie sort of chuckled to herself like that was a joke.

Sarge watched as Pickett and Maggie brought over four mugs full of coffee and sat down. The last fifty-some years had not been friendly to Maggie, that was for sure.

Maggie asked the first question. "Are you the detectives who found Connie and her boyfriend and Katie and Kevin and Becky Williams?"

"We are," Pickett said.

"Thank you," Maggie said. "I always worried that they might be down there, but couldn't imagine why they couldn't get out."

"Were you down in the speakeasy with them?" Pickett asked.

Maggie shook her head. "Didn't know they had gone down there. I had gone in the day before and took a picture and then left. Place really creeped me out, let me tell you."

Sarge sighed softly. That explained the only evidence they had and the picture. And Maggie's voice was surprisingly strong coming from such a feeble-looking body. And clearly her mind and memory seemed to be crisp.

"Why did you go down there alone?" Pickett asked turning to face Maggie across the glass kitchen table. Robin and Sarge stayed back.

Maggie laughed. "I was dealing with two books that had chapters about the place and wanted to know if it existed or not. So I called a friend who worked on maintenance at the casino and he told me about the locked door and told me how to find it and gave me a key he thought might fit. The door turned out to be right where Harrison said it would be. So I got curious."

"Harrison show you his map?" Pickett asked.

"I had it with me, actually. And a camera and a flashlight that wasn't bright enough by half."

"That tunnel must have been something," Pickett said.

Maggie just shook her head at the memory. "Scared me something awful. And dusty, wow. And beyond creepy. Felt like I was walking back into time."

Sarge could only agree with that, but both he and Robin both stayed silent and let Pickett keep up the questioning.

"So you took a picture?" Pickett asked.

Maggie nodded. "Pulled out a few chairs from a table, staged a couple bottles and glasses on it, and got back in the corner and took the picture with a flash. Put all the stuff back, then left. Never so glad to be out of a place in my life."

"What did you do when you got out?"

"Went back to my office and put Harrison's map back in the file, then went home to take a shower and change clothes. I think I might have had a few drinks that night to try to clear out that memory."

"Did you tell Connie that you had found the place?"

Maggie shook her head. "I never saw her or her boyfriend or Harrison's friends Kevin and Katie again. I assumed Kevin and Katie had gone home and back to college and that Connie and her boyfriend Rusty had gone down to San Diego. I remember he had a lead on a job there. When we realized she was missing a few weeks later, we searched San Diego and reported her missing there."

"Did you read about the search for Becky Williams?" Pickett asked. "Did you think she might have been trapped in the speakeasy?"

"No way to be trapped in there," Maggie said, shaking her head. "All you had to do was go through the tunnel to get out. So I knew something else had happened to her, until I read the paper about your find."

"Did you ever think about Harrison's claim there was money down there?" Pickett asked.

Maggie laughed. "Sure did, every time my husband and I got a little tight on the money. But there was no chance I would ever go back down there. For any amount of money, even if I knew it was there, which I am still betting I would be wrong on that."

The three of them said nothing about the fact that she would lose that bet.

"Why didn't you publish Harrison's book?" Pickett asked.

"Because even though he and his wife were brilliant, it was all speculation except for the speakeasy and even the main focus of that, the money, was speculation. And one small part of a large book just wasn't enough to make it work. Our company focused on historical facts, not wild treasure hunts."

"Why did you leave Connie's book alone?" Pickett asked. "Even after you had seen the place."

"Connie never came back, so I put in the picture and labeled it in the 1930s to show that Connie's research was solid. Not my place to start a treasure hunt in that newly remodeled building. I figured that someday someone would find the place. Didn't think it would take over fifty years, though, and never thought Connie or anyone else would be down there, not with that tunnel to get out."

Pickett nodded and looked around at Robin and then at Sarge for any more questions.

Sarge believed the story Maggie told. It all made sense.

"I have one question," Maggie said. "The papers said they were found dead in the speakeasy. Can you tell me how they died? The all didn't really think they were trapped in there, did they?"

There was a sound of almost horror in her question, imagining her friends suffering for days in the dark.

Pickett said softly, "They were murdered."

"Murdered?" Maggie said, softly, looking directly at Pickett. "Why? Who would do that to such nice kids?"

"That's what we are trying to figure out," Pickett said.

And Sarge nodded to that because his worst fear had just come true. They were right back where they started. No clues, no suspects.

Nothing.

Part Six

SO THIS IS WHAT SQUARE ONE LOOKS LIKE

CHAPTER FORTY-FIVE

February 4th, 2023
Las Vegas, NV

Pickett and Sarge rode in silence after leaving Maggie's home. They both believed her, as did Robin. And Maggie never really had a motive to kill her friends.

Pickett just kept thinking back to those five mummified bodies slumped over and around the table, down there for over fifty years waiting for someone to find them. And the one person who had actually been in the speakeasy the day before had no reason to believe anyone could get stuck down there with the tunnel entrance so easy to use.

To be honest, Pickett would have felt the same way.

And now they knew the killer had not gone out of the speakeasy through the tunnel. So more than likely the killer had gone up through the apartments. Going through the tunnel there would have been another set of tracks.

Unless there was a third way into that place they had not found yet.

Damn she hated that thought.

They had decided to have lunch at the deli in the Circa Casino on

Fremont Street, so Sarge pulled into the parking garage and they waited for Robin to join them and they all headed in without really talking.

The deli on the second floor was welcoming, with high ceilings, light music, and lots of comfortable places to sit. Plus it had some of the best deli-style sandwiches of any place in Vegas and that was going some.

Once they had ordered and were seated in a back booth away from everyone, Robin broke the silence. "I assume you two believe Maggie?"

Sarge nodded.

"Maggie had no motive to kill them," Pickett said. "So yes, I believe her, and I was looking in her eyes as she answered my questions and she was telling the truth. I think honestly, she felt relieved to finally talk about it to someone."

Both Sarge and Robin nodded.

"So back to the start," Sarge said, shaking his head. "We have no idea who killed those five people and why. No fingerprints, no footprints in the tunnel, nothing."

"A third way into the place, maybe?" Pickett asked. "Sure, our killer could have gone up through the hotel, but with the intense search for Becky Williams starting the next day, someone would have remembered someone unusual when she went missing."

"A third entrance?" Robin asked.

Sarge sort of nodded. "That was a lot of booze down there. Hauling it in through the hotel tunnel or the hotel above the speakeasy would have drawn attention from the Feds at the time."

Robin just sighed, then said, "Can we finish lunch before I call poor old Baker and ruin his day again?"

Sarge laughed and said, "Sure."

"We will need Heidi as well," Pickett said.

Robin and Sarge both nodded. Pickett really hoped they wouldn't need The Cowboy this time for another tunnel.

"I had hoped to never see anything but a picture of that speakeasy again," Robin said, clearly not happy.

Pickett wasn't happy with the idea either. But all the way along they had been grasping at straws. This was just one more.

At that point the large sandwiches arrived and thankfully, for a short time, all three of them were too occupied eating to talk.

CHAPTER FORTY-SIX

February 4th, 2023
Las Vegas, NV

One hour later they were standing outside the main construction area of the remodeling of the Independence. To Sarge, he couldn't see much progress at all other than the former front door had been expanded out large enough to drive a truck inside.

The sky was clear and deep blue like it got sometimes in the winter, and the wind was light, but even so the temperature wasn't that comfortable and the sun had no power of warmth at all.

Pickett had explained to both Baker and Heidi her idea and told them that they had cleared the person who made the footprints in the tunnel. So they were now thinking that the killer got out through a possible third entrance.

"A supply entrance to the speakeasy?" Baker asked, frowning.

Beside him, Heidi from the historical society and Mob Museum sort of nodded. Then she said, "It was not unheard of for a speakeasy to have a hidden supply entrance. And you are right, with that much supply down there, going through the Independence Hotel or the one on Fremont would have never worked to keep the place stocked."

"Damn," Robin said to herself.

"I remember that on the picture of the neighborhood you showed us," Sarge said to Baker, "there were a number of homes close by. Were any of them owned by Sanderson?"

"I can find out," Baker said. He turned and started toward his construction trailer.

"Hang on," Heidi said. "I can look it up on my phone. Finding the speakeasy got an army of researchers going over this entire area."

The four of them stood there in the rapidly cooling afternoon and waited as Heidi looked up the ownership information of nearby homes back when the Independence was built.

Then she shook her head and put away her phone. "Sanderson owned both of the nearby homes to the east of the Independence."

"The back wall of the storage room is on the east side," Sarge said.

"Damn it," Robin said.

"Once more into the past," Pickett said, shaking her head.

Sarge just said nothing. He had zero desire to go down into that death room again. But since they had no other clues to go on, they needed to.

Baker gave them all a helmet and turned and lead the way, with Heidi at his side.

There was a guard on the entrance in the basement to the speakeasy and Baker had two of his men help with opening the heavy concrete blocks and then block them open until they came back out.

Baker and Heidi lead the way down the stairs. Clearly to them this wasn't a murder room, but an exciting historical discovery.

Pickett and then Robin followed and Sarge brought up the rear.

When Baker turned on the lights, Sarge looked around again. The door to the outer area was propped open and all the chairs and tables had been wiped down, along with the bar. All the bottles of booze remained on the back shelves in front of the mirrors and the wall hangings all looked like they were about to fall.

Basically it looked like a ruin from the past with furniture and a lot of dark brown bottles.

"Heidi," Sarge asked. "Why are all the bottles brown and unlabeled? Is that normal for a speakeasy?"

"There was no normal when it came to the booze," Heidi said. "Often the bottles were green and had some sort of label on them, but these came from the San Francisco area and the gin had green corks and whisky had brown. The bottles were made to use to pour water on passenger ships."

Sarge nodded.

"Money still back there?" Robin asked.

"Nope," Heidi said. "All moved to a safe location for sorting. The owners of the property and the historical society and Mob Museum came to an agreement on how to split the final proceeds. It will be a great deal when all finished."

"Collectable or actual," Robin asked.

"Actually both," Heidi said, smiling. "For example, once this is fixed up and opened to the public, we'll sell Lucite encased twenty-dollar bills for hundreds. Only one of the many ways that money will serve this place."

"Including paying for the restoration," Baker said.

Sarge was very glad their discovery would end up being something of pleasure eventually. But right now they had to find who killed the five people back in 1971.

He turned for the door into the back room, which was propped open. Baker followed him and turned on some overhead construction lights that had been hung over every row of bottles.

Sarge could not believe the amount of booze that was in this room.

He went to the wall on his right and then walked along the shelves of bottles to the back wall.

Pickett walked down the row beside him and Robin took the next one over.

Robin found the entrance behind an odd shelf and a large wooden cask-like barrel that was empty.

Together, with Baker's help, they got the hidden door open and shined their flashlights down what had been a tunnel. Twenty feet in the entire thing had collapsed.

"Looks like that was purposefully destroyed," Baker said, staring at the pile of dirt and rubble. "Look at the explosion signs on the wood."

Sarge could see what he was talking about, but he would love to have The Cowboy take a look at it.

"Footprints?" Pickett asked.

They all got down low in the doorway to the hidden tunnel and let the bright lights from their phones illuminate the layer of dust on the floor between them and the destruction. It looked almost exactly like the dust in the tunnel headed downtown.

"No prints," Robin said.

"This tunnel was more than likely destroyed when Sanderson shut the place down," Baker said.

"Killer didn't get out that way then," Sarge said, snapping off the light on his phone and heading back toward the main room of the speakeasy.

And once again they were at square one.

And flat devoid of any ideas at all.

CHAPTER FORTY-SEVEN

February 4th, 2023
Las Vegas, NV

Sarge had gone out into the main room of the speakeasy and pulled a chair out at a table near the bandstand and sat down. Pickett followed, sitting beside him. Thankfully the tables and chairs had all been cleaned, more than likely when they were moving the money out.

Across from them was the table of death.

Robin came out and joined them.

"Not ever going to get used to this place," she said.

"Never want to see it again," Sarge said.

Pickett totally agreed. But there was clearly something about this place they were missing. More than likely the killer had gone back up into the apartments above and no one noticed him or her. And if that had happened, after this many years, the chance of tracking that person down would be laughable.

Basically, they were finished. Pickett knew that just like the ghosts in this room, this case would haunt all three of them.

Robin had her head down. Sarge was just staring at the bar. And

Heidi and Baker were still talking in the storage room about the new find.

Suddenly Sarge stood and said, "Pickett, Robin, join me at the bar."

He went around behind the bar and Pickett shrugged at Robin and they both pulled up a bar stool facing him and the bottles of booze and the mirror. The way the light was, their reflections sort of looked like ghosts.

Sarge pointed to an empty spot on the second shelf and then an empty spot on the lowest shelf just above the back bar area.

"This is where the two bottles the five drank came from," Sarge said. "Right? Looks like they just randomly picked two."

"That is the supposition, yes," Robin said.

"Heidi," Sarge said a little louder. "Could use your help on some history."

A moment later Heidi and Baker came out of the back room and stood by Pickett. Heidi looked puzzled and Pickett just shrugged. She had no idea what Sarge was thinking, but she knew enough over the years they had worked together to let him go when he had an idea.

"In most speakeasys were all the bottles identical like these are?"

Heidi nodded. "Moonshine was moonshine for the most part. No reason to have different bottles unless the maker ran out of a certain type of bottle. It was either gin or whisky of some sort that could be made into all kinds of different drinks."

"And you said some speakeasy booze makers had labels?" Sarge asked.

"They did," Heidi said. "Collectors go crazy trying to get a certain type of Prohibition bottle from a certain area. These will all have a collector's value, even though they look the same and there are a lot of them."

"Put on your crime scene gloves," Sarge said and pulled out a pair and put them on.

Pickett handed Baker and Heidi each a pair and then put hers on, as did Robin.

Sarge carefully took a bottle off the middle shelf and sat it in front of Pickett and Robin. It had a faded green cork, so it was gin.

"See the black mark near the top?" Sarge asked.

Pickett stared at the neck and sure enough it was marked with some sort of black mark that had faded over the years.

Sarge went to one end of the shelves and pointed out as he went down the bar that all the bottles on the bottom shelf and second shelf had a similar mark. Did not matter their color of cork.

Then Sarge stood on his tiptoes and managed to get a bottle off the top shelf.

"No mark," he said.

He sat that bottle away from the other two and turned to Baker. "Could you select a random two bottles from the back room and bring them out?"

Pickett looked at Sarge with a puzzled look, but he indicated she should just wait. A moment later Baker came back with two bottles.

"No marks," Baker said, putting the bottles on the bar and turning each one so everyone could see.

Sarge just nodded and turned to Robin. "Would you call Andor and get a forensics team and active detective down here as soon as possible."

Then Sarge just stood there smiling.

Suddenly Pickett understood where Sarge was driving at. The marked bottles were all poisoned.

"Sanderson?" Pickett asked.

Sarge just smiled even bigger and nodded. "I'm betting he poisoned the bottles to protect the money."

"I'll be go to hell," Robin said. "He didn't want to ruin all his stash of booze, so he marked the poisoned ones."

"Exactly," Sarge said as he carefully replaced the marked bottle where he had found it and the unmarked to the top shelf. "Our murderer couldn't leave tracks or be seen leaving. He was already long dead before he killed those five."

CHAPTER FORTY-EIGHT

February 4th, 2023
Las Vegas, NV

Baker and Heidi went back upstairs to wait for the detective and forensic team and Pickett and Sarge and Robin went back to the table near the bandstand to sit and wait. Warmer down here than it was upstairs or outside, that was for sure.

To Pickett, suddenly the place didn't feel so bad. And she could see that when it was remodeled and cleaned, it would be an amazing tourist attraction. She still didn't want to come back down here again, ever.

"How did you even think of all the bottles being poisoned?" Robin asked Sarge.

"Motive," Sarge said. "Protecting millions of dollars was a motive to kill the members of that band." He indicated where the instruments still sat, waiting.

Pickett just stared at them. She had a hunch the historical society would put up the band members names in large letters behind each of their positions.

"And Sanderson had to know that a lot of people knew how to get down here," Sarge said. "And could guess about the money. So I'm betting he figured that if someone wanted to try to break in to take the money, it would make them thirsty."

Pickett stared at the rows of poisoned bottles. She had to look really hard to see the faded black marks.

"How did you see the marks from here?" Pickett asked.

Sarge laughed. "I didn't. I noticed them when I walked the length of the bar looking for where an entrance to the secret room would be. Figured it was just a way to mark what had been opened or something. Forgot about them until we were sitting here."

"Well," Pickett said, "if the tests show that they are all poisoned, we can put this one to bed."

"I'm betting Sarge is right and that they are," Robin said.

"I know they are," Sarge said. "Because otherwise we are flat out of options."

"So," Pickett said, "a man who had been dead for thirty-six years reached out of the grave and killed five innocent kids. Now that's a first for my career."

Robin laughed. "I think pretty much for all of us."

CHAPTER FORTY-NINE

They hadn't had a meeting with Robin at the Main Street Station buffet for almost an entire week, so Sarge was actually looking forward to the breakfast and maybe an extra dessert or two.

And to find out what new case Andor had given them this time.

It had taken two days for the results to come back that all the marked bottles had been poisoned. None of the others had been. Sarge's theory was spot on the money.

And that more than likely it had been Sanderson who had put in the poison, more than likely the day after the bar closed to protect the money he never lived long enough to spend. His fingerprints were on his guns and also on all the poisoned bottles.

The case was ruled solved and closed.

Twelve deaths because of that money, but now it was going to be spent wonderfully, not only to help make the remodeling of the Independence even nicer, but to help the Nevada Historical Society and the Mob Museum grow.

Sarge and Pickett had stopped by and talked with Connie's brother, and then they had seen Maggie and told her as well the entire story. Both were very appreciative.

Even though the news of the money had not been released yet, they stopped and told Harrison that he had been right about it. And then he and Sarge talked about the lost mine up in the red rocks. It was a fun visit for Sarge, but not so much for Pickett.

So now the sun was out, the temperature just cool enough for a light jacket, and no wind. The five-block walk from their condo was just perfect.

Sarge just felt great to be back working after the long layoff and he felt even better walking with Pickett, laughing and enjoying the day. And was really enjoying the feeling of success in solving a really tough case.

This morning a good breakfast awaited he and Pickett and a new cold case from the task force. That excited him.

And there might even be a few pieces of pie.

What wasn't to like about the morning?

USA TODAY BESTSELLING AUTHOR

DEAN WESLEY
SMITH

A DOC HILL THRILLER

DEAD
MONEY

""[An] exhilarating political poker thriller."
—*Midwest Book Reviews*

If you enjoyed Case Card, *you might enjoy the book that inspired the entire Cold Poker Gang Mystery series,* Dead Money. *The following is a sample chapter from that book.*

THE GAME BEGINS

PROLOGUE

Poker is not a game of cards. It is a game of people.

Central Idaho Mountains. August 17, 2009

Silence.

Silence, the absolute worst thing a pilot can experience at seven thousand feet in a single-engine Piper 6XT. A moment before, the engine had filled the cockpit with a solid rumbling, a vibration-filled sound that Carson Hill knew from hundreds of hours of flight time.

The engine-monitoring system panel hadn't given him a warning. The plane had shaken with what had felt like a small explosion. Then everything on the control board had just snapped down to zero. Black smoke had poured out of the engine compartment, covering the front windows with a thin, black film.

Now the smoke was gone and through the film he could see the tree-covered ridgeline directly ahead.

The slight creaking of metal, the faint sound of the wind rushing past the six-seater's windows. Nothing else broke the deadly quiet.

He forced down the panic threatening to overwhelm him.

"Goddammit! What the hell happened?" His voice seemed extra loud.

He took a deep breath. Losing control now would just make sure he died.

In his hands, the plane's controls felt heavy, unresponsive. His dead-stick training was from a book and a few sentences from his original flight instructor over three decades ago. He had never actually flown a plane without a working engine.

Around him, the dark blue September sky contrasted with the green forests and brown rocks of the Idaho wilderness below. Normally, he loved this easy flight. He'd done it every year at the same time for longer than he wanted to admit. Now everything below him looked like a night-mare in the making, ready to reach out and tear him apart.

The ridgeline loomed ahead, a wall of death. He wasn't clearing that ridge.

He forced himself to take a deep breath. Then, with shaking hands, he fought to get the plane into a very slow turn.

Nothing wanted to move.

The trees ahead filled everything in his sight.

He kept fighting the controls, forcing the plane to turn by almost sheer will. It took every bit of his strength, as if the plane had a mind of its own and actually wanted to crash into the trees and rocks.

Everything seemed to slow down.

Finally, the trees were no longer growing threats filling his vision, but instead were flashing past the wing's tip.

He bet he didn't miss the tops of the pines by more than a few feet.

Somehow, between deep, sobbing breaths of oil-tainted air, he got the plane leveled and back over the deep valley, headed downstream. Sweat ran down his face and into his eyes as he tried the restart sequence.

Nothing.

With almost no control, no engine, no place to land but into trees and rocks, he was as good as dead.

He pushed that thought away and grabbed the radio mike. "Mayday! Mayday!"

Silence.

No response from either the McCall or Cascade, Idaho airports.

He clicked on the global positioning emergency beacon. At least Search and Rescue would find him quickly.

Ahead, the narrow valley floor closed down tighter and tighter. He couldn't be more than a thousand feet above the stream and dropping faster than he wanted to think about. It was taking every bit of his strength to keep the plane flying and not stalling.

He wiped the sweat off his face with his sleeve and tried to get a good look at what lay ahead through the oil-smeared window. Sharp rocks and thick forests covered everything. At this speed, and without any real control, the plane would be torn apart on impact.

"Need an opening," he said. "Just give me an opening." His voice sounded loud and strained in the silence of the cockpit.

The valley narrowed ahead into a rock canyon, but over the edges of the rocks he could see a meadow beyond. If he could make the meadow, he might have a chance.

He tried to focus on the open area where the sun was shining, pushing the plane past the dark shadows of the rock canyon and into the light.

But he was dropping far too fast.

He tried feathering the controls to keep the plane up, but nothing seemed to work. Instead of something responsive in his hand, it felt like he was pushing against a stuck handle and pedals.

The rock walls now loomed ahead, a tiny opening leading to the sunshine beyond.

It was going to take a lot of luck to fit the plane through that narrow canyon opening. And after thirty-three years of playing professional poker, he didn't much believe in luck.

Then, quicker than he realized possible, he was in the canyon, the rocks flashing past. Ahead, the meadow seemed to call to him, the bright sunshine a beacon.

A tip of one wing caught the rock cliff face.

Before Carson had time to react or even cover his head and face, the small plane slammed into the rock wall.

Steven leaned against a tall pine in the shade, trying to stay cool, watching impassively as Carson Hill's plane struggled to stay in the air.

From Steven's position on the top of the major ridgeline dividing the Cascade Valley from the central Idaho primitive area, he could see clear to the Middle Fork of the Salmon over thirty miles away. He had picked the spot just for that reason.

The day had turned beautiful, almost hot. He had waited patiently for six hours, slowly drinking bottles of water, until the signal had come in from the device he had planted in Carson's plane that told him Carson had started up his engine at the Scott airstrip deep inside the primitive area.

Steven felt no emotion as Carson Hill's six-seater Piper Cub barely escaped crashing into the hill below him. He simply watched as the plane drifted silently down the valley. Carson was full of all kinds of surprises. He shouldn't have been able to make that turn, not with his engine gone and his controls damaged in the small explosion Steven had set off in the plane's engine compartment.

The hillside below Steven had been the intended crash sight. More than likely the crash would still kill Carson, but it wasn't going to be close enough for Steven to retrieve Carson's key.

Steven shrugged. That was only a slight glitch in his plans. Too bad. He had wanted to take the key from Carson's dead, mangled body. There would have been a nice justice to that. But there would be other keys to give him that pleasure. There had been ten players in that poker game. Nine keys.

Steven dropped the small remote detonation device he had used to set off the explosion in Carson's plane into a three-foot-deep hole he had dug while waiting, then quickly filled the hole back up, covering it with pine needles. No point in carrying the device back down the mountain with him. No one would find it here, and even if they did, it couldn't be traced to him. He had left no detail to chance.

He trusted no one.

He had learned that lesson well.

Carson's key would survive the crash, and even with Carson dead, someone would have the key very shortly, then take Carson's position in the game.

If Steven had to kill that person, as well, so be it.

NEWSLETTER SIGN-UP

Follow Dean on BookBub

Be the first to know!

Just sign up for the Dean Wesley Smith newsletter, and keep up with the latest news, releases and so much more—even the occasional giveaway.

So, what are you waiting for? To sign up go to deanwesleysmith.com.

But wait! There's more. Sign up for the WMG Publishing newsletter, too, and get the latest news and releases from all of the WMG authors and lines, including Kristine Kathryn Rusch, Kristine Grayson, Kris Nelscott, *Pulphouse Fiction Magazine, Smith's Monthly,* and so much more.

To sign up go to wmgpublishing.com.

ABOUT THE AUTHOR

Dean Wesley Smith

Considered one of the most prolific writers working in modern fiction, *USA Today* bestselling writer Dean Wesley Smith published far more than a hundred novels in forty years, and hundreds of short stories across many genres.

At the moment he produces novels in several major series, including the time travel Thunder Mountain novels set in the Old West, the galaxy-spanning Seeders Universe series, the urban fantasy Ghost of a Chance series, a superhero series starring Poker Boy, and a mystery series featuring the retired detectives of the Cold Poker Gang.

His monthly magazine, *Smith's Monthly*, which consists of only his own fiction, premiered in October 2013 and offers readers more than 70,000 words per issue, including a new and original novel every month.

During his career, Dean also wrote a couple dozen *Star Trek* novels, the only two original *Men in Black* novels, Spider-Man and X-Men novels, plus novels set in gaming and television worlds. Writing with his wife Kristine Kathryn Rusch under the name Kathryn Wesley, he wrote the novel for the NBC miniseries The Tenth Kingdom and other books for *Hallmark Hall of Fame* movies.

He wrote novels under dozens of pen names in the worlds of comic books and movies, including novelizations of almost a dozen films, from *The Final Fantasy* to *Steel* to *Rundown*.

Dean also worked as a fiction editor off and on, starting at Pulphouse Publishing, then at *VB Tech Journal*, then Pocket Books, and now at WMG Publishing, where he and Kristine Kathryn Rusch serve as series editors for the acclaimed *Fiction River* anthology series.

For more information about Dean's books and ongoing projects, please visit his website at www.deanwesleysmith.com and sign up for his newsletter.

For more information:
www.deanwesleysmith.com

f facebook.com/deanwsmith3
▐● patreon.com/deanwesleysmith
BB bookbub.com/authors/dean-wesley-smith

Printed in the USA
CPSIA information can be obtained
at www.ICGtesting.com
LVHW042153100923
757617LV00009B/170/J